SECRETS AT THE GAS STATION

Sarah Kaldor

Published by New Generation Publishing in 2022

First Edition

ISBN

	Paperback	978-1-80369-425-2
	Ebook	978-1-80369-426-9

www.newgeneration-publishing.com

New Generation Publishing

The Book Challenge

WHAT'S YOUR STORY?

This book was published through
The Book Challenge Competition part of
The London Borough of Barking and Dagenham
Pen to Print Creative Writing Programme.

Pen to Print is funded by Arts Council, England
as a National Portfolio Organisation.

WHAT'S YOUR STORY?

Connect with Pen to Print
Email: pentoprint@lbbd.gov.uk
Web: pentoprint.org

ARTS COUNCIL
ENGLAND

Supported using public funding by

Barking &
Dagenham

Dedication

Thank you to: Carole and Peter Kaldor, Denis and Linda de Winter, Ruyter Suys, Conrad Wood and Ian Ayris who's help and support was invaluable during the writing of the novel.

CHAPTER ONE

The gas station stood alone in the middle of the flat lands of the prairies of America outside a town whose name escaped even itself. It was a lonely day in a lonely place, the chitter chatter of last night long passed. The station manager - his ideas of the world based solely on what he found in the Enquirer magazine - had tried to find adventure in the same bar he had frequented for at least 10 years, but came away, as ever, with nothing.

The gas station had two pumps standing regimented side by side waiting for the call of action, like seasoned army cadets. Like an old married couple, they comfortably sat in silence and got on with their tasks.

After a light trickle of teenager cars had filled up for an evening of activity that tried, but always failed, to be exciting, a blot on the landscape pulled up to herald the start of an unbusy day. An elderly man with white and grey hair got out of the uninspiring, clunky car, filled up with gas and went up to the checkout window. He paid, got back in the car and meandered off into the distance. This short burst of activity briefly ruffled the shirt of the station manager and the gas pumps, for some unknown reason, but was soon forgotten. On closer inspection, seen only by the insects that gathered there and the gas pumps themselves, it was seen that the man had lodged a white envelope in the space between the gas pump nozzle and the gas pump.

But nobody listens to gas pumps or insects, so the station manager remained unaware.

A few hours passed by with only flies for customers.

A car in the distance brought a young couple in the middle of a road trip - a short vacation to break up the monotony of their daily lives by having coffee served to them in remote surroundings, rather than serving it themselves in the unceasing activities of the city.

'I'm really hungry now,' complained Dara impatiently. 'There was a Taco Bell back there, we should have stopped.'

'I thought you didn't like Taco Bell,' replied Ruben sarcastically. 'Too *inauthentic*, you said.'

'No, *you* said that,' replied Dara.

'Yes, but it was you who wanted the whole "diner experience".'

'I know, but not if it meant starving. You said there was one close by.'

'There is. According to the map there should be one any time now, near that gas station.'

'Give me that!' said Dara, snatching the map from Ruben.

Dara studied the map. The diner seemed close on the map but there was nothing in sight. Then she looked at the map again and leaned over to Ruben.

'Look, the motel's still about three or four miles away,' she said. 'On this map that's practically next door to the gas station!'

'It looks so close on the map with nothing surrounding it,' said Ruben sulking. 'They might have something here. If you're that hungry, let's see.'

Ruben went to pay with the excitement of getting on a bus to go to work. A road trip? They were both over it.

When Dara picked up the gas nozzle from the pump, the envelope fell to the ground. Dara picked the envelope up without intrigue as though it should be there. She watched Ruben and the station manager exchange a few words, her concentrated boredom broken for a moment and instead of placing the paper back where it came from into the hole where the nozzle goes, she put it in her bag. Realising Ruben might be ordering food she ran into the kiosk to join him.

'It looks awful,' she hissed quietly at Ruben hoping the man behind the counter wouldn't hear.

The man behind the counter was nonplussed and answered Dara as though she had spoken directly to him.

'If it's a good feed you're after then there's diner down the road, five minutes drive from here.' He pointed out of the window in the direction of the only road in sight. Dara and Ruben's gaze followed the direction of his forefinger and looked baffled at the sight of nothing at all.

'Just right there,' the man said, sensing the puzzlement of two strangers obviously not from round here, 'where the sky meets the earth.'

Dara noticed a spec on the horizon.

'That's it,' said Dara in sudden realisation.

'That in the distance is five minutes away?' said Ruben in disbelief. 'It seems so far away.'

'As the crow flies,' said the man. 'It's about three miles.'

'There's nothing to see round here,' the man continued. 'Not like you city folks where you can't see more than ten feet in front of you without some three mile high piece of steel in the way. Here there ain't nothin' but the sky above. Nothing in the way to block the view apart from a few birds here and there.'

Ruben and Dara edged out of the kiosk.

'Thanks,' said Dara

'That's great to know,' added Ruben as he shut the door behind them.

The bell tinkled briefly, announcing their exit.

'They really ain't from round here,' said the man to himself before completely forgetting about them.

Ruben started the car.

'So there's a diner fifteen minutes drive from here,' he said. 'So what are we waiting for?'

And off they went.

After a while, Dara remembered the envelope and got it out of her bag. It was heavier than she first thought. She opened it and pulled out a piece of paper folded around two keys. One side of the paper said: *These keys open the gate which opens the box – whoever finds it you must open it and bring back to this place what you find inside.*' She turned the paper over. 'And look,' she said. 'This side has got some sort of diagram on it and some writing in a foreign language.'

She read the note to Ruben.

'Aww, Ruben, we must go back. It might be part of a child's game... I feel bad for taking it.'

'No way', said Ruben, 'I'm too hungry. Anyway, what children? It's just silly. Throw it out and don't be so ridiculous.'

But Dara held onto it. Something made her curious. A spark of interest on the horizon breaking up the tedium of driving long distances. It was probably meaningless, like Ruben said. But what if there was something to it?

Keys are made to open something, she thought. But what was that something? Trying to find out would at least give her something to do on their long journey to nowhere.

The rest of their drive to the diner whistled on with the open car windows making for the only breeze, the only sound the hum of the car engine. Even cheap cars these days are too smooth to complain about the lack of interest on a long-distance journey. From the start of their life in the factory, there is no story of the treachery of being born into poverty or the dependability of being rich with the loyalty of money. No chance of a journey into the opposite state through fate or by actions. Just the slight discomfort of being just about comfortable, but always with the sense that something was missing.

Eventually, Dara and Ruben reached the diner, and pulled into the pointless parking lot.

'This must be it, the illustrious diner,' said Dara

'You mean illusive,' said Ruben

'That too.'

They both got out and stretched their legs and arms like puppets being taken out of their boxes, and entered the diner. The diner was large and mostly empty apart from a waitress, a chef, an old man and his dog. It looked to have been part renovated many years ago, the more mundane aspects of 50s décor looking more tired than historic. The rest of the original features, probably replaced some time in the 80s. Ruben looked around at the décor in distaste as Dara sat down.

'Sit down so we can order,' hissed Dara, beckoning Ruben over.

'Oh god,' snarled Ruben. This 80s version of the 1950s is so bad. They should have left the originals in.' He flicked a piece of the table that had just chipped off when the buckle of his belt caught it as he sat down. 'And look. The whole place is coming apart.'

Dara studied the menu: 'Ooh look at this,' she said, and pointed to a garish picture of a burger with bacon poking out the sides and a bottle of maple syrup standing at an angle next to it. 'The house burger. 'Half breakfast and half lunch'. That's what it says here.'

'House burger? Where are we?' said Ruben. 'Some sort of French restaurant? What makes it breakfast and lunch, anyway?' he added, more as a statement and only half curious. He really couldn't care less, but on the other hand he did wonder what sort of a person would do that.

'It's with bacon and maple syrup,' said Dara with a genuine excitement at the thought of something slightly exotic.

'Their food is as confused as their décor,' said Ruben. 'But a burger is a burger and French fries are French fries. All American food.'

'What else are you gonna get in a diner,' said Dara looking for the waitress. 'Just order something,'

The waitress suddenly appeared at the table.

'That's two house specials,' said Ruben.

'Great,' said the waitress, weirdly excited. 'It's been a while since anyone ordered one of those,'

And she trotted off to the kitchen.

The inactivity and boredom of a long car journey, and the plain hunger of them both caused the food to go down easy.

When they'd finished, Ruben paid the waitress, Dara went to the adjoining store next door to get some provisions for the next leg of their journey. At the counter, she took the paper out of her bag as she searched for her money to pay the cashier.

'What's that?' said the cashier, pointing to the side of the paper with the strange diagram and foreign words, adjusting her hair which had fallen out of its clip in order to see better.

'I found it at the garage,' said Dara. 'What do you think it is?'

'Well, that shape is familiar, look at this.' The cashier produced a local paper. 'We had a crop circle like that about a year ago.' The lady flung the paper on the counter and pointed.

'Alien visitation, they say. If you find out what they want let me know. The name's Rosemary.' Rosemary studied the writing. Dara hadn't taken a closer look before.

'It looks like it might be German,' said Dara.

'It is,' said Rosemary, snatching it out of Dara's hand to look at it more closely, not expecting to be surprised. 'My parents were German. I speak German. Not since my mom died, mind, but it's still there.' She looked even more shocked.

'See here, it says Lufthansa. That's an airline. And it says something about tickets to Berlin.'

'Tickets?'

Dara dug the envelope from her bag and emptied two tickets onto the counter.

'And here,' continued Rosemary, 'it gives you the passwords to get into the webpage and add your name. And here's an address. Mind you, it has to be used in five days' time!'

Ruben came into the store to see what the holdup was, breaking the bond that had suddenly grown between Rosemary and Dara over the random piece of paper that had come into their lives. He had overheard the last part of their conversation and, although he had started to become intrigued, he wanted to keep up the idea that it was all nonsense and nothing to do with them.

'Not that again. I thought I said it was better to throw it.'

'But it's two plane tickets to Berlin, Ruben! A free ticket to Europe!'

'No-one gives away free tickets. It's a scam. A joke. One day we will go and do it properly, with a tour bus, I promise.'

Rosemary continued to read. 'It says here you will be given $4,000 in Berlin and a further $50,000 on return!'

Dara and Ruben were stunned. It must surely be a joke.

The usually conservative and unimpulsive Ruben started to fantasise about taking up this unexpected offer and going to Berlin. Despite looking African American, half his black roots lay in Berlin. His grandmother, although black, was born in Germany and met a Jewish German soldier stationed in Berlin. So surprised was he to find a black Berliner, his grandfather became infatuated. Ruben's father had made sure Ruben understood his heritage, and Ruben often wondered how his grandparents had got through the war living in Nazi Germany. Ruben might have relatives living there still. He was so measured in life that Ruben kept putting the fantasy out of his head but it kept creeping back in. What if? And perhaps now was the opportunity. And all that money? Perhaps it really was now or never.

Dara, however, was not so enthused any more. There is no such thing as a free lunch, as they say. To offer so much money for what was essentially an international courier gig. Her friend had done this kind of thing before. He'd gone to France to collect some jewellery for some rich lady who didn't want to get it in person. Her friend had only been paid five grand for this job. This extra zero made Dara wary. For that amount the stakes must be high. She sensed danger with that amount of money. Danger money reminded her of mobsters, but this cryptic message didn't seem to be gangster style.

Dara returned everything to the envelope, and led Ruben to the back of the shop out of earshot of the cashier: 'It would be so cool to go on an adventure,' she whispered.

'I dunno,' said Ruben. 'It's very suspicious.'

'You're right,' said Dara. 'I told you about my friend before. And how he got paid five grand to bring that jewellery back'

'Oh you would have a friend who did something like that,' replied Ruben. But it got him thinking. If someone else did it, why couldn't they?

Both pondered over that last statement.

'Anyway we'd better get going,' said Ruben.

Dara turned and said goodbye to Rosemary, and they left the diner.

Ruben and Dara strolled out to the car in silence.

It was Ruben's turn to drive.

After some hours there was a rare turning off the road. Ruben did something quite unexpected. He couldn't say why. An existentialist moment, he thought later. He felt compelled to break out of his comfort zone. Because what was his comfort? Working in a job that doesn't need his expensive college degree? Doing the odd rare job as freelance graphic designer? Sending out resumes? Continuing to make coffee for a living? As he drove along the long road to nowhere (the next town) he thought about where his studious, consistent reliability had got him.

Absolutely nowhere.

Ruben turned off the road and headed to the airport.

He had decided.

They were going to Berlin.

CHAPTER TWO

Dara had been living in Atlanta a while. She had landed there after a brief stint at the Savannah College of Art and Design, thinking she might want to get into TV. It was close to where she grew up and she immersed herself in the centre of the Little Five Points district. Dara and her friends, Tamara and Jackie, spent their days wandering around over-priced vintage stores, their favourite being the mad and bad Junkman's Daughter and their nights in the mad bars, gritty and grimy, open to 4am. Dara loved both the nightlife and the day life.

Tamara was lucky enough to get a job at the Junkman's Daughter after she graduated. She first met Dara there when Dara was buying a pink wig and a pair of cut-off denim shorts, along with a rubber eyeball and some shiny black latex trousers.

'I'm going to a Cramps gig,' said Dara to the shop assistant.

'Cool,' Tamara said. 'The one on Saturday? I love the Cramps. Didn't manage to get a ticket, though.'

'I have a spare ticket you can have. My boyfriend's not going any more.'

'That's amazing! Thank you so much. Why's your boyfriend not going,' asked Tamara.

'He's not my boyfriend anymore.'

A voice came from behind a rack of striped T-shirts.

It was Jackie.

'Hi, I'm new in town,' Jackie said. 'I don't really know anyone and I'm going to the show too. Can I tag along?'

'Sure,' said Dara

'Bless ya heart,' said the facetious Tamara at the unassuming Jackie.

The gig was the first of many the three of them would go together.

Tamara soon lost her disdain for Jackie and the three of them began to drink together at the Vortex where Tamara's boyfriend worked. The familiar greeting of the huge open-mouthed skull which acted as the doorway to the Vortex was the entrance to the belly of the beast of junk food and booze, constant gurgling drunk chatter and people milling around crashing into things. It became a familiar and comforting presence. Clinking beer bottles or cocktail glasses, the three of them talked about clothes, boys and music. Sometimes they bought clothes with Tamara's discount, hooked up or went out with boys and listened to live bands at The Star Bar, like the 45s or Nashville Pussy. Nashville Pussy had badass women playing guitar who hung out in the bar afterwards.

Eventually, Dara got a part-time post at The Junkman's Daughter when her crappy job at Starbucks reduced her hours. She lived for her new job, surrounded by vintage clothes and listening to music with Tamara, rather than counting down the hours and minutes at Starbucks. But what she really longed for was to work at the way cooler café next door to the shop.

Tamara was an exuberant customer and sometimes too over the top for Ruben. But her friend who recently started accompanying her to have a coffee next door, seemed more measured, as well as being part of the zany crowd. It was hard to have demure friends in this city. Those he'd gotten to know often dragged him along to whatever antics they got up to. They were always trying to set him up with someone unsuitable, such as the day he first met Dara at the Vortex - the tackiest bar he'd ever seen.

'Going fishing today?' Ruben's friend, Harrison, said to his other friend, Mackenzie.

Harrison glanced at Ruben and the rest of the group with a sharp look to show he meant them too, a look that conveyed he wanted an answer. The others obeyed and started making banal and sexist comments.

'Over there by the window,' said Nolan. 'I've not seen her before.'

'That's Crazy Durk's niece,' said Austin, a wealth of local knowledge. I wouldn't even look unless you want to end up at the bottom of the quarry. Remember Thomas's brother, from when we were kids? They say it was Durk, how do you think he got his name? Thomas took his sister out on a date and thought he would tell Durk about it. Durk was not pleased. A neighbour heard a glass smash and some raised voices before a car engine started and rumbled into the distance. Never saw Thomas again.'

'Yeah, right,' said Harrison, cutting Nolan off before the story got too clichéd. 'Thomas was seen after that in town, he took a trip after one too many, that is all.'

Ruben tried not to get drawn into their remarkably simplistic comments and take on the process of finding a female partner. It was what people did, one of the few motivations in this dusty town devoid of any other meaningful activity. Ruben knew this was his friends' way of searching for their significance in this world, so Ruben tolerated it. But they wouldn't let Ruben off the hook in their conversation. Just their way of trying to be inclusive, he guessed.

'Ruben?' said Harrison, waiting for the answer.

'What ah, oh I don't know. Don't ask me.'

'But we do,' replied Harrison. 'You're one of us, a buddy, part of the team.'

'For someone who hates Communists, you guys really have a sense of communal togetherness, the basis of Marxist theory,' replied Ruben to the esteemed fraternity.

'What?' said Mackenzie. 'I ain't no Commie!'

The others looked blankly. Ruben dropped the subject. Now was not the time. Their minds were on finding a partner, even if it didn't last (it never did), with which to set up home and live on a street interacting with their neighbours in their own suburban commune.

In order to change the subject, Ruben scanned the room for someone to show interest in. In doing so, his gaze came across someone intriguing, though he couldn't say why. At the bar stood a tall young woman with short dark shiny hair, her white skin a contrast to her mainly black attire. She somehow fitted the surroundings without being part of it. Her clothes were muted and different from the others. No garish pink and yellow pastel and no make-up, no frayed, faded denim shorts or crop top - all of which Ruben saw as an expression of the faded, fraying town, full of abandoned houses laid bare, built for an industrial age leaving nothing but an imprint of what could have been on the present day. This girl wore dark jeans and a black top with a silver abstract shape which gave her the intrigue of a black and white photograph.

'I'm going over there,' Ruben said, nodding to where Dara stood at the bar. Ruben wondered at his sudden change of heart. The guys nudged each other as they watched Ruben, noting the gaze in his eyes, so left their standard jokes at Ruben's usual lack of enthusiasm.

'Where,' said Harrison, turning his head this way and that, scanning the joint.

'There by the bar,' answered Ruben, 'The girl with the silver bits on her t-shirt.'

'Looks like a serial killer,' said Nolan. 'You know, like in *True Romance*.'

'What are you talking about, Nolan?' said Ruben snappily, standing up and leaning across the table as he spoke. Mackenzie pulled his arm to indicate he should sit down.

Austin saw in the girl what Ruben saw, though. A thoughtfulness and depth as though if you went inside you'd find more than her size showed. A living tardis.

'Dudes,' he said. 'Keep it calm. You're not dating her yet.'

Ruben sat down in a huff.

'Well, it'll make a change from the last one you set me up with who thought Cosmopolitan was a book,' Ruben retorted as he sank back down into his chair.

Harrison waded in, in an attempt to defuse the impending spat.

'Why don't you go over then. Get the drinks in while you're there.'

For once, Ruben didn't think this was a bad idea.

'If you don't walk up to her in the next 5 minutes I'll carry ya,' added Mackenzie.

In an uncharacteristic moment of spontaneity, Ruben seized the opportunity and went over to the bar.

'You come into my café don't you,' he said. 'The Aurora.'

'Yeah,' replied Dara, recognising Ruben as one of the employees from the cafe next door to where she worked.

'Well it's not my café,' Ruben continued, before Dara got the wrong idea. 'I just work there.'

'I don't own Starbucks either,' replied Dara, slightly sarcastically. 'I work there,' she added. 'As well as the Junkman's Daughter, which I also don't own.'

Both paused, and giggled slightly.

'I guess neither of us own anything,' said Ruben, breaking the silence.

'No, I guess not,' said Dara.

There was another pause. Dara looked over at Tamara and Jackie.

'Nice to meet you,' she said, then turned and started to carry the drinks she'd ordered back to the table Jackie were sitting at.

Jackie got up and met Dara half way: 'What are you doing? Don't leave him, he seems into you. It's about time you moved on from that schmuck.'

Jackie always sounded unconvincing when she used Yiddish slang, even though it was now part of the general vocabulary. There was an urgency in Jackie's voice Dara didn't often hear from her, only if she was dead sure about something.

So Dara turned back.

'Where are you from?' Dara said, appearing as if from nowhere in front of Ruben, who by now, always quick to judge and defeatist, had cut his losses.

'What?' he replied, having to shout over a group of people who had congregated at the bar

'What?' Dara replied, unable to hear him over the squawking crows pecking at each other over drinks and what kind of French fries they wanted.

Ruben leaned in close to her so she could hear. 'Let's go outside,' he said, guiding Dara around the single, out of place chairs, tables that people had abandoned for a moment. He stretched out his arm around her shoulders without actually touching them and she moved with him.

Once outside, the chatter faded as though on mute. They sat on the ground, bottles in hand.

'I was asking where you were from,' said Dara.

'I'm from Connecticut,' said Ruben. 'Kind of boring.'

'So what brings you here?'

'I ended up at Savannah State. Mom wanted me to go. She went there. She's smart, *really* smart but you know those times were different. It gave her the opportunity to develop her intellect which she's tried to pass onto me. She wanted me *to remember my roots in the oldest, most prestigious traditionally black college in America*, said Ruben, as if quoting his mother's wishes.

'What did you study?'

'History of arts and social politics.'

'Sounds big.'

'My dad's Jewish, son of an immigrant escaping Europe. Dual heritage of oppression, gives me an interest in social politics. The art's just for fun, and it helps me to think. Or it's one of the two, perhaps both.'

'Why are you still here then? I mean this place is hardly the epicentre of high octane culture.'

'I don't know, it has a certain vibe. The people, the craziness of Little Five Points. They're fun to be around. There's life here. And Little Five Points sure beats Connecticut. Connecticut is too suburban, everyone's so sedate, I need to see life. LA's more lively but there's an empty undertone which doesn't sit right with me. Everyone chatters and is friendly, *too* friendly. One moment they're talking to you, the next they're ignoring you like you don't exist, like they forgot their script that day.

'What about NYC?' said Dara. 'Have you been there?'

'It's too quick,' said Ruben. 'Too much pushing and shoving. And the quick-thinking talk-back of New York is too much for me. I like to walk along the road without feeling like I'm in the eye of a whirlwind. You can find peace and quiet here. I got a part-time job at the Aurora café during my studies, and I thought it was so cool. An independent café with books, so 90s Seattle. I'm old fashioned, so after I finished studying, I just kinda stayed. Didn't know what else to do, I suppose. What about you?'

'Nothing to tell really,' replied Dara, not wanting to give too much away, thinking her life so small compared to his. 'I come from San Diego. It's okay here, I suppose. Nothing too out there. I love the chilled-out pace of life - less hectic than New York and less obsessive than LA - and people talked *to* you in Atlanta, unlike *at* you in the Big Apple or *through* you in LA. You know what I mean?'

Ruben smiled and nodded, and took a swig of beer.

'What about school?' he said?

'Majored in Media at SCAD. Thought I might get into TV but I don't think my smile was fake enough, I don't see the point in loving everything, you know? My classmates were so enthusiastic, I'm not sure they thought I was. But they didn't really know me. They looked cool but they were cheerleaders in disguise. I guess I just didn't fit in. I did art as well – sculpture, metalwork - that was fun. I didn't have to talk to anyone. But I guess that won't get me a job, though. Not a proper job. I got a part-time job at Starbucks, who reduced my hours, then eventually I wangled a second job at the Junkman's Daughter. Right next door to the Aurora. We've been there a few times - me and my friends. That's where I recognised you from.'

Dara had the feeling she was revealing too much, and made her excuses and left to join her girl pals. Ruben was awakened. Metal-sculpting was rad, and this girl was fascinating. He wondered what her apartment was like. What things she had, what she read, what she did.

Somehow one day, Dara and Ruben got together at a Bigfoot gig, started dating and when Dara got kicked out of her apartment, she moved in with Ruben. Both groups started to intertwine. Even though they didn't always have much in common, Ruben enjoyed Dara's cool popularity and Dara felt more intelligent with the bookish Ruben. Somewhere along the line, the demure Jackie even got together with the boisterous Mackenzie, each cancelling each other's extremes out or taking on some of each other's characteristics until they met in the middle.

Domesticity followed. Shopping trips to Kroger, their nearest was Mexi Kroger but Ruben like Jewish Kroger as he felt his affinity there seeing all the kosher food, even though he wasn't kosher. Murder Kroger, nearest to Little Five Points was best avoided and sometimes if Ruben was cooking a special meal and wanted good wine, he'd swing by Gay Kroger. And so it continued.

Their life wasn't unpleasant but it was becoming a little repetitive.

CHAPTER THREE

Berlin may as well have been the moon and the rest of the world the sun. Dara had travelled a few times to Mexico (though couldn't remember much about it). But that was it. No relatives in exotic places apart from an uncle in Colorado. She drifted through high school trying to avoid the high-pitched voices of the boys and girls who wore the uniforms even though uniforms were not part of American school life. Most of them drifted past her, perhaps stopping for a moment to stare at this foreign object if she got in the way, tall and sullen, before screaming excitedly about seeing their friends, for the millionth time. No one could understand her lack of ambition or lack of interest in joining in anything at all.

But she wasn't the only one. There were others too. She wondered what happened to some of them.

Her friend Mary was in New York studying photography at the School of Visual Arts. She visited Mary once whilst still a student. Unlike Mexico, she had vivid memories of this one adventure. They went to bars, they went to gigs. The buildings were the tallest Dara had ever seen, and the place was so cold. People wore more black than she'd seen before, complementing the grey buildings. They looked more like her sort of people. But only in appearance. They acted like time was running out. They needed things now. They needed to do things immediately, perhaps it was the cold and this was their way of trying to keep warm. Perhaps she was more like Atlantans than she realised. One outing with Mary included a spoken word performance, people telling their stories in rhythm or telling jokes that are funny but don't make you laugh – but people laughing anyway. Another time there was a fight and glass smashed all over the floor.

Dara kept meaning to visit Mary again but, as yet, the thought had not made it into an action. She wished for a moment she had studied there too but there was fun to be had in Atlanta. She didn't run from experience, but maintained a distance. Somehow, though, snippets of life found her.

Ruben, on the other hand, had been everywhere but nowhere. As a child, he went with his parents from LA to San Francisco. The blinding California sun shone from the streets through the windows and onto his books as he studied. As a kid, playing volleyball on the beach only appealed as an activity in his mind, as did rolling down the hills of San Francisco in a cart. By the time he got to Connecticut, he realised what he'd missed. But it was too late now. He travelled to many places in the pages of the books he read. North, South, East and West. He followed the adventures of Shackleton to both Poles. He even went to 19th Century France and Tudor England - the lively narrow streets of Paris and London as real in his imagination as those outside his front door. He did remember briefly visiting London as a child with his second cousin on a visit with his mother, though, it rained and so he stayed inside most of the time. He watched the people walking in the rain, chattering, like the teeming rain were rays of the sun. Ruben was fascinated by their optimism in trying to find the sun, even though it wasn't there, but going out anyway.

Dara drifted through community college with a passing interest in media, arts and literature, before carrying on her part time job in the non-descript chain coffee shop, full time. She had hoped to hear the conversations of politics and intrigue like the coffee houses of the romantic past, but all she heard was whinging and gossip from blandly dressed former yuppies and some lonely ex-students pretending to work on laptops. When the coffee shop reduced her hours, finally she took a leap of faith and landed a job at the Junkman's Daughter - the hippest place in town - selling ideals of the past instead of the promise of nothing but a cup of coffee.

But now she was actually going somewhere. Into the unknown. To Berlin. If the past is a foreign country, she thought, then Berlin is certainly the past - especially on the east side.

Dara had never been to an airport. On the few occasions Dara had travelled, she went interstate on a Greyhound bus. Even to Mexico she drove along the coast with the girls, taking it in turns to sleep and drive, staying over in a motel with only one bar in town - a night she'll never remember. She had really only seen airports on TV or in Films.

As Ruben and Dara checked their cases through security and check in, Dara felt guilty, but didn't know why. She was apprehensive, as though someone was about to unveil a secret that even she didn't know about. She felt like an intruder. People like her didn't travel to far away places. Ruben on the other hand seemed in his natural habitat going about the checking-in procedure with the ease of ordering a coffee at Starbucks. Airports are really one giant shopping mall with the promise of goods free of duty, he'd told her.

'Do you want Burger King?' he said, the red and yellow burger sign shining bright a little way off. Then Ruben realised their tickets were business class. He was so excited.

'Forget that,' he said, before Dara had a chance to answer. 'These tickets are business class. They've got a special lounge.'

'Cool, free food,' replied Dara. 'I bet it'll be good.'

They showed their tickets to the woman at the desk, who looked at them for a moment before letting them in. It was clear Ruben had also never been in a business class lounge before as he looked around in wonderment, staring at how unremarkable it was.

'Is this it then?' he said.

There was one other passenger in the room, seated at the far end. Dara went over to him to see what she could discover.

'Where's the food?' Dara said to the man.

'Drinks are over there?' the man said, indicating to the middle of the room where a trough of alcohol stood. Wine

19

bottles in ice, vodka, four types of whisky, gin. You name it, it was there. Dara thanked the man and returned to Ruben.

'Where's the party?' said Dara, sarcastically.

'It's morning,' declared Ruben. 'This really does move forward the notion of "daytime drinking".'

'Shall we go back outside?' said Dara, 'You know where there's life. This place looks like it is in need of a party. This bar would be great if only it wasn't in an airport. It's like it's been delivered to the wrong place and left to rot.'

'Nah,' replied Ruben. 'Let's stay here. It's still business class.'

Dara and Ruben sat and read the free magazines. Dara had a Jack and Coke just because she could. Eventually their numbers came up and their flight was ready to board.

Being a Lufthansa flight, everything was distinctly unexceptional. They got on the plane. They sat in their seats. Announcements were made over the tannoy, and the plane slowly eased out of its parking spot like a bus with wings. On this occasion there had been a slight delay and airplanes were waiting to take off. Dara looked out of the window and there she saw literally a queue of planes, as though waiting their turn at a drive through.

The plane turned the corner and Ruben couldn't help feeling they were about to do the same. There was nothing special about being in a passenger plane and taking off. Inter US flights were cheap and the easiest way to get from one city to another in this vast country - a country almost the size of Europe. After take-off, Dara had a feeling of unease. Until now she pretty much knew where she was headed in life, what she was doing, even in her drift-like state, and even if things did not turn out as expected. This time, however, she had no idea what was at the other end of this particular line. Ruben, by contrast, the one who was always nervous about what was going to happen next, actually felt a sense of calm. Though he did have more of an idea of what to expect and what he was going to do whilst in Berlin. Both had almost forgotten the actual reason they were going.

Upon landing at Schönefeld airport, Dara and Ruben stood in the short line for non-EU citizens. They stood in relative silence, lost in their imagination, passing comments about feeling hungry, or what the food was like on the plane. It was a way of not worrying about what they might find when they got to the place they were due to stay, and what they were supposed to do next.

'I need the bathroom,' said Dara.

She found the sign for the toilets and tried the door. But the door wouldn't open. She went to the customer information desk and told the women behind it.

'The door to the toilet is locked,' said Dara.

'No it's not,' the woman behind the desk said, no surprise or questioning curiosity in her voice at this strange phenomenon.

This confidence flummoxed Dara: 'Yes it is,' she replied, questioning her own sanity. She went over to try again, but again it would not open. Dara returned to argue her case.

'It is locked,' she said again.

'No, it isn't,' came the same reply, the woman not moving from behind the counter to even check.

Dara wandered around and eventually found another entrance to the toilet.

Okay, she thought. But why didn't the person behind the counter check and why didn't she think of saying there were two entrances? Things were sure different here.

Dara was beginning to wonder why she'd come.

'What was with that woman,' said Dara to Ruben. 'I said the door was locked and she didn't believe me. She didn't even come out to check.'

'Perhaps she was too busy to come out.' Ruben smiled, adding, 'Or perhaps she wasn't wearing anything on her bottom half'

'Stop kidding,' cried Dara. 'This wouldn't happen in the States. People would complain. She must know the airport, why didn't she tell me there was another door. Why didn't she say? Where's the customer service?'

'It's just the way they are,' Ruben said. 'Direct and to the point. People don't complain here, they just get on with things. It's just their way.'

'Well, I don't like their way. I'm beginning to wish I was back in Atlanta where life is simple. All I had to do was go to the store and fold some clothes and go to my other job and make coffee. I mean what am I going to do now? What are *we* going to do now? We haven't even been outside the airport and already things are different. The people, the shops, the food. And this place is so small. Even the Coke can is different. How are we going to cope with whatever we're supposed to do next? Especially when we don't even know what it is!'

This sudden outburst was out of character for Dara, and Ruben began to worry about her and what they had let themselves in for. He was beginning to have his own fears about what exactly they were going to do, aside from why they thought to come in the first place.

'Remember,' Ruben said, gently, 'just the other day when you were moaning about how boring your job was and how you did the same thing every day?'

Dara nodded, putting her head on his shoulder.

Ruben put his arm around her and continued. 'Well, this is our chance for something different. Different is what we wanted. We do not know what will come next. We don't really know what will come next back home, we can only guess. But we are here now and there's no going back even if we wanted to. Nothing bad will happen, it can't. We just need to keep moving forward until we get there.

'Get to where?' asked Dara.

'We've got the address where we're supposed to go,' replied Ruben. 'That's a start. And then when we get there, I'm sure it'll all become clear.'

This all got Dara thinking. At least this sentimental philosophy redirected her mind and brought her back to the task at hand, distracting both their minds temporarily from the fact they really didn't know what to expect next, perhaps for the first time in their lives When you expect things to stay the same you can cope with sudden change as it is the anticipation of the unexpected that leads to fear. After all, nothing out of the ordinary had ever actually happened to them.

Ruben examined the piece of paper with the address written on, but decided to ask a passerby to be sure.

'Do you know how to get to Schönhauser Allee,' asked Ruben to the stranger.

The stranger seemed in a hurry but answered anyway before scuttling off.

'You need to change at The Alex,'

Ruben was really none the wiser, but set out on their journey anyway down the stairs and got on the next train out of the airport. To his delight, Ruben saw Alexanderplatz subway station or U-Bahn as it was called on the train's route map and deduced that this must be what the hurried stranger had meant by 'The Alex'.

When they arrive at Alexanderplatz Ruben lead the way, exiting the station.

'I just want to see something before we go down to the subway,' he said to Dara.

Dara grunted: 'fine,' as she didn't have much choice not knowing where she was or how to get to the next destination.

Outside in the light of the breaking dawn, the vast square was empty of the bustling centre for life of its historic past. But out of the sky, glistening in the sun was a tall needle shaped building.

'That's what I'm here to see,' announced Ruben. 'The Fernsehturm, the tallest building and they eye of the Communist media. It's just a broadcasting tower but a symbol of power.'

'Ok, very impressing, can we go now?' said Dara walking toward the nearest U-Bahn sign. 'I'm fed up with dragging this suitcase around.'

The subway station itself had so many entrances, and had a huge central space. As it was early in the morning the station was deserted, still waiting for the commuters and tourists to emerge through the cracks of this historic interchange. Despite this, it wasn't a calm space and had an underlying menace that made it seem smaller than it was. The lights were dim but you could just make out the dirty walls and floor. So different from the New York subway which had the ever presence of activity no matter what time of day or night. Even when empty, the colourful graffitied walls seemed to be in constant flux each time they were cleaned or added to.

There was a lonely set of ticket machines in the middle of the main entrance. Dara tried to navigate them but struggled to work out what to do. A youngish man in his early 30s asked if she needed help, immediately speaking English to her. Dara declined his help, and shook her head, not wanting to engage with him and hoping he would go away. The man wore a well-worn tan brown leather bomber jacket and pale blue jeans. Very out of style in the states. She wondered if she'd just flown back in time. The man paced around the station for a bit before going up one of the staircases to the street. Ruben, meanwhile, was still coming down the staircase on the other side of the entrance, struggling with his suitcase and disturbing the quiet with the clunks of his efforts.

CHAPTER FOUR

Having worked out the ticket machine, Dara and Ruben headed for the escalator and got on the train they needed. The train was empty. There were plenty of people but not enough to find yourself in close proximity of a stranger as in New York - the only other town either of them had experienced an underground network. No-one was yelling, as they always did on the New York subway. Dara noticed there was no interaction at all, friendly or violent. No-one even spoke. It was as though the passengers were trying not to notice one another in case something dreadful might happen if they did. The atmosphere rubbed off on Dara and Ruben, and neither of them spoke for fear of breaking the silence. It made Dara feel self-aware of every movement and noise she made. A cough, her breathing, the movement of her head - all became magnified as though all parts of the train would hear and come to a screeching halt and spit her out if she made a sound.

A man stared suspiciously at Dara, as though he knew she shouldn't be there, and that his next act would be to report her to some higher authority on the train. Dara looked away and found herself looking at a middle-aged woman in a beige raincoat. The woman looked up briefly but quickly looked back down again, staring at her fingers, as though she didn't want to be caught and reported to the invisible power either.

The journey seemed to go on forever. Even if the train became stuck in a tunnel, Dara realised they wouldn't know what to do and she would be too afraid to ask for help.

Ruben sat with his head bowed, holding onto his suitcase as though trying to hide it under his arms. He lifted his head to say something to Dara, but thought better of it, lest he might be heard. He glimpsed the woman in the beige raincoat fiddling with her hands but didn't look any more in case he saw too much. When no-one moves, the slightest twitch is noticed from far away and becomes a curiosity. If no one speaks the curiosity becomes suspect, something to mistrust rather than a thing of wonderment.

As the map had indicated, they got off at Eberswalderstrasse station. The place seemed a bit busier and more like a station. The station was above the ground on stilts with many exits to choose from with steep stairs down to different parts of the road.

'Which set of stairs do we go down,' asked Ruben, as though Dara would know.

'How should I know?' Dara looked at the map, indicating points on the map with her finger. 'If we are here and we want to be here, we want to go there so....'

'Let's just choose one' said Ruben, taking control, convinced he would know when they were on the street, where to go. So down the stairs they went to street level. They turned left for no educated reason at all. Dara followed Ruben, and they walked, and walked and walked, lugging their luggage behind them on wheels that didn't always turn.

'God this is so heavy,' moaned Dara.

'Keep moving,' hissed Ruben. 'I'm sure we're almost there.'

'We've been walking for ages, are you sure we are walking the right way?'

It was then they saw Pankow station, the end of the line, they realised they had come out the wrong way. It was the other left. So back they went, past the where they started and carried on.

'I knew it' hissed Dara. 'Let me look at that map.'

'I was following you,' Ruben said.

'No you weren't. And don't blame it on me. And, anyway, I was following you. I thought you knew where you were going.'

'How could you be following me when you were in front?' argued Ruben.

'No I wasn't.' replied Dara in a huff.

'But you didn't stop me.'

And so they kept on walking. In the right direction this time.

An hour or so later, Ruben brightened considerably. 'This is it,' he said, not quite believing it himself.

Schönhauser Allee 152. Apartment 7 was 5 floors up.

'Oh you have got to be kidding me,' moaned Dara. 'Seriously, there's no elevator? There must be! How is this possible?'

'It's an old building. And no, I can't see a elevator anywhere.'

'What is this place?' said Dara. 'They really don't like to make life easy for themselves here, do they?'

'It's Europe,' replied Ruben. 'Like I said before, they don't complain or sue you for the slightest thing, like back home. They just get on with it. Perhaps they should complain. But I guess it's not in their nature.'

They tugged and pulled at their gear to the first landing.

'I long for my first floor apartment now,' said Dara. 'I'll never complain again about having to go up one flight of stairs.'

'The trick is not to try to do it all at once,' replied Ruben. He put his bags down on the landing and, starting with Dara's case, carried one case up each flight, and came down for the next. Then the other and then the bags. Soon it was done, and Dara and Ruben stood outside the apartment door.

'See, teamwork,' said Ruben, a little breathless. 'Like a workout at the gym.'

'Have you got the key?' said Dara.

Ruben pulled the key from his pocket. It looked like it came from an older world than this, like it should open an antique box. But it was just a door key.

Once inside the apartment, Ruben and Dara both looked around for any indication or clue as to why they were there. But it was just an ordinary apartment. Through the door there was a lobby with a bedroom to the right, a bathroom to the left and a door ahead. Through the door was a large living room going off to the right with a balcony, though it was too cold to go outside. The open plan kitchen was to the left. New, modern with light wood and glossy granite surfaces. Ruben - suddenly overcome with exhaustion - slumped on the sofa that was against the wall in the middle of the living room whilst Dara checked out the kitchen.

'There's a coffee machine,' said Dara, half excited. She fiddled around a bit but couldn't work out how to use it. She opened cupboards, finding her bearings. Eventually she found a lonely packet of tea. Mint tea.

'Want some tea?' she asked Ruben.

'Yeah, sure,'

'It's mint,'

'Whatever. Just about anything will do.'

Whilst Dara was in the kitchen, Ruben noticed a brown padded envelope by the television set on a wooden table against the wall opposite, and brought it back to his place on the sofa.

'Look what I found,' he called out to Dara.

Dara came in from the kitchen.

'Open it,' she said. 'It might be important.'

Ruben opened the envelope and pulled out a wad of cash.

They stared at each other, open-mouthed.

'This must be the four thousand,' said Ruben.

'Which means . . .'

'Yep, Dara. This thing is real.'

They looked at each other in silence, eventually broken by Ruben.

'So,' he said, 'is that mint tea ready yet?'

Dara made a cup of tea for each of them, and tried to figure out how to use the coffee machine. Eventually she found a cafetiere in one of the cupboards, much easier to use.

'What about food?' asked Ruben, expecting Dara to know what to do.

'I know, I'm hungry too,' she replied. 'The only thing I can find is this flyer for a pizza take-out place.'

'That'll do. I will eat just about anything,' replied Ruben.

Dara was thinking the same thing, so she rang the number.

'How do I do this, I don't speak German,' she said.

'Just ring, see what happens.'

Dara rang the number: 'Hi, do you speak English?' she asked.

'Yes of course,' said the voice on the other end. 'What would you like? We have a special offer, if you buy two you get a free bottle of Fanta.'

The guy at the other end almost spoke better English than Dara, who had no idea what a Fanta was. She didn't want to appear stupid, so just said, 'Okay.'

Dara ordered a Margherita pizza for herself and Ruben's favourite Hot 'n' Spicy Chicken.'

'Will you be paying by cash?' asked the man on the phone.

'Yes,' said Dara, remembering they had cash.

Meanwhile, Ruben turned on the TV. After pressing a few buttons he found Netflix. The pizza was delivered shortly after. They might not complain here, but they sure were efficient.

Take out pizza, Netflix – suddenly everything became familiar again. Watching a film, Dara and Ruben fell asleep.

The next morning, Dara awoke early and made some more mint tea for them both. The whole thing felt like waking up from a dream. After all the recent activity they were suddenly still, but in unfamiliar surroundings, wondering what had just happened. As she made the tea, Dara saw an antique looking saucer on the floor, broken into pieces. It was a sort of willow pattern but in a vivid blue. She was sure it wasn't there yesterday, and hoped Ruben hadn't accidentally smashed a priceless piece of crockery. But he would have said something, surely? She picked up the broken pieces of the saucer and put them on the counter, thinking about how she might put it back together.

'What's that?' Ruben asked, coming into the kitchen and pointing to the broken crockery on the countertop.

'I found it on the floor. Why didn't you tell me you'd broken it, Ruben? It could be expensive.'

'I didn't break it,' Ruben said, defensively. 'And anyway it's only cheap.'

'Well if you didn't...?'

'Dara,' Ruben groaned, 'you do like to make up stories, it's just some junk.'

With that, Ruben gathered up the broken pieces of saucer in his hands and threw them in the trash can. Dara was irritated for some reason, but thought he was probably right.

A little later, when she was throwing the teabags in the bin, Dara noticed some of the saucer pieces were turned upside-down, and there seemed to be some pattern or writing on the base. She got the pieces out of the bin, laid them on the countertop and put them back together like a jigsaw puzzle.

The writing spelt out: KFOAHFCHTIaAHrT0.

Obviously some nonsense, Ruben said.

As always, Dara thought he was probably right, but something niggled her about it and she put the pieces in the cupboard to examine later.

CHAPTER FIVE

Ruben and Dara almost felt uneasy in each other's company, both thinking the other mad for getting them into this situation. Within the space of just a few days they had gone from cruising along in the USA to finding themselves in an apartment in Berlin wondering what on earth they were doing there. None of it seemed real. But here they were, looking out onto strange streets where crocodiles once roamed.

Gazing out of the window, Ruben imagined uniformed soldiers marching up and down looking for something out of line, and he shuddered.

'What you looking at out there?' asked Dara, waiting for an answer to see if it was worth joining him at the window.

'Nothing,' replied Ruben. 'Just thinking about those streets out there seventy years ago. There'd be uniformed men marching up and down, keeping order and rooting out undesirables hiding in the shadows. The permanent noise of shouts and screams and gunshots. It's so quiet now, as if none of it ever happened. Swept under the concrete so no-one would even know.'

Dara went to the window and looked over Ruben's shoulder, then returned to the kitchen.

'Being Jewish, I'd be screwed,' Ruben continued, as if almost to himself, 'and being black too, I'd have had no chance. I would have had to hide in a basement, or worse. And you too, Dara. You're part Jewish, aren't you?'

'Catholic, if anything,' replied Dara. But yes my grandmother used to say she was part Jewish. She said her father - my great grandfather - was from Poland, or Hungary, or somewhere. Maybe even Germany. Someone escaped or survived, or something. I don't remember the full story. But the Germans wouldn't have done anything to her, unless she joined the resistance, I suppose.'

'Yes they would,' Ruben replied. 'All you needed was one great grandparent who was Jewish.'

'That's ridiculous. How would they know?' said Dara.

'Meticulous paperwork. Modern civilisation runs on bureaucracy. They didn't need Google in those days.'

'Hah?' Dara thought for a moment. 'That is a scary thought. So what happened to the black people in Germany back then?'

'Like in the States, I'd imagine. But that's what I'm here to find out. My mom told me my grandmother survived by singing.'

'Is that right? You never said,' replied Dara

'No-one ever really understands when I talk about it - what it feels like knowing what my family must have gone through, so I don't bother. None of it is featured in the history books,' continued Ruben. 'Perhaps I'll write something one day.'

Ruben turned away from the window and closed the net curtains.

Dara, still in the kitchen area, came out and put two cups of mint tea on the coffee table in front of the sofa. Ruben sat on the sofa, collecting the teacup from the table as he sat down. The teacup had a saucer with it so Ruben hesitated awkwardly before picking up both, holding the saucer in one hand and the handle of the cup in the other.

'So, what are we going to do?' he said.

'Dunno, wait.... for something, I guess.'

Dara sat down beside Ruben, her feet up on the coffee table, and the two of them did nothing all morning. The silence was only broken by the distant sound of a French horn. Dara wondered about it briefly, but Ruben, drowsy from the last evening's events, hardly registered it.

'Can you hear that?' said Dara

'No, what?' replied Ruben.

'That sound. Some sort of horn, I think.'

'Strange to hear someone playing something like that here. Perhaps they are practicing.'

'What for?'

'Who knows?' replied Ruben. 'I wish I knew what piece it was.'

'You have to know everything. It's just some music.'

Ruben breathed deeply but didn't reply. 'It's something to do,' he said.

It was getting close to lunchtime and Dara was getting hungry.

'What are we going to do for lunch?' asked Dara

'I dunno, not thought about it,' replied Ruben. 'I'll think about it later.'

Dara was irritated at Ruben's lack of action, but didn't say anything.

'Fine, I'll go out and get something from the store. There must be something around here,' she said.

'Okay, great,' came Ruben's reply. 'Want me to come with you?'

'No.'

'You sure?'

'It's best if one of us stays here. Just in case something turns up,' replied Dara.

The truth was she needed the break, tired of the constant compromising one does when in another's company. She wanted to be in her own thoughts, just for a while.

'I suppose so,' said Ruben. 'And, Dara, see if you can get some coffee. I can't stand any more of this mint tea.'

Out on the street, Dara felt as if she was going hunting in a post-apocalypse movie. There were not many people around - just the odd one or two spread out along the wide streets, walking alone. Dara wondered where they were going, what they could be doing and longed to ask. There didn't seem to be much around in terms of food shops. There were buildings and random businesses, but most appeared to be closed. One shop sold just wooden toys and another lace curtains. Eventually she came across a small health food shop and bought some pasta, some rice and tinned tomatoes. All these were familiar, similar to what she could buy back home. The bread, however, was much darker and more dense - so dense it was impossible to squeeze. The loaves sat there on the shelf, uncovered, open to the air.

Dara bought apples and some spinach leaves, potatoes and carrots. She marvelled at the cheese section. None of the cheeses on offer was what she was used to. She had no idea what she was getting so she picked something that looked tasty and hoped for the best.

When Dara returned, Ruben was still sat on the sofa. 'Why did you take that broken saucer out of the trash?' he said.

Dara had forgotten to mention her discovery. 'Where is it?' she said.

'I put it back in the bin. Why would you put it back in the cupboard? I put it back in the bin. It's trash.'

'It's not, Ruben. I noticed something.'

Dara took the shopping to the kitchen, and came back with the pieces of the saucer in her hand. 'Look,' she said.

Ruben screwed up his face like a child trying to recite a times table at school that he had forgotten as she laid out the pieces of the saucer on the coffee table.

Ruben was less surprised than Dara thought, considering how unusual it was to find some kind of code on the back of a broken saucer.

'I know this!' exclaimed Ruben, after looking at the combination of letters for a moment. Then the memory that so nearly poked its head round the door in his brain went back in and slammed the door shut. 'No, it's gone.'

Ruben decided to make lunch to see if the memory would come back if he concentrated on something else. He enjoyed a bit of cooking and loved those cooking programmes with Gordon Ramsay. Perhaps he would try his hand at being a chef one day. He looked through the items Dara had salvaged from her shopping trip and made a simple pasta dish with a tomato sauce, and sautéed the spinach. To his delight, Dara had bought some cheese, which - like Dara - he didn't recognise, but went with it and grated some over the top of the pasta. All in all it looked like a picture.

They'd not really eaten anything apart from junk food or airport sandwiches for some time so the taste of vitamins from earth grown veg was intense and flavoursome. Even the pasta tasted different. At least it tasted of something. As far as Dara was concerned, this meal made up for everything.

'What shall we do now?' asked Dara. 'First things first,' Ruben said. 'Coffee.'

Dara smiled. Ruben and his coffee.

As Dara made the coffee, she found herself constantly wondering what they ought to be doing, something she never really did back home. Back home, she knew where to go, who to call, where everything was. Here she had a burning need to do something but didn't know how to go about it. She looked to Ruben for inspiration, but Ruben usually went along with whatever Dara did.

Dara came in with the coffee.

'So,' she said. 'Here's your coffee. So, what next?'

'I'd like to explore the city,' Ruben said. 'Look at the sights. The Brandenburg Gate, the museums, Radio Berlin, Checkpoint Charlie. Get it all in before the storm. Potsdam, Alexanderplatz, if we can. Oh, and Karl Marx Allee.' Ruben paused for breath as if readying himself to add to the list.

'I'd love to see the wall,' Dara said. 'I mean I just can't picture it, in the middle of a city, a wall. Where'd they put it, aren't there houses or apartment blocks right on it?'

'We're twenty years too late for the actual wall,' joked Ruben, 'but there's a museum and photos, I think they left part of it up as a reminder. My college roommate went there as a child. He showed me some photos. On the western side, every inch of the wall was graffitied. I remember him saying how weird it was. You walked down what should be a normal street and suddenly there's this thing in the way and over the other side you can see the same apartment blocks. The wall wasn't even that tall - only about twelve feet, so you could see the taller buildings rising up on the other side. Everything was so close yet completely unattainable. He said the wall was the physical barrier, but it was like there was an invisible forcefield rising right up to the sky preventing all kinds of communication – unless you wanted a spray of bullets. He said it was like the wall wasn't really there, like it was just an illusion, like something in a computer game. He had a way with words. I think he wanted to be a writer, or journalist or something.'

'There's some flyers here. This must be the Brandenburg Gate,' said Dara looking at a photo on the front of one of the flyers aimed at tourist attractions. It doesn't look like a gate. Where's the entrance? It looks like a monument, some columns.

'Here's something that looks cool,' continued Dara pointing to a flyer with a photo of a cobbled street and café tables. 'Looks like the local bar. *The White Russian* in Kreu.... Kreuz.'

Ruben took the flyer. 'Kreuzberg,' he said. 'It's closed now though. But it says on the back there's a café, look: *The Honey Pot Cafe*. I'd like to explore that area anyway. It's part of the old East Berlin. It's where all the cool kids hang-out. Apparently. The happening place. My friend said the old East Berlin was like Williamsburg back home. Let's go there, Dara. we can walk around and chill in the café. It'd be almost like we never left home. Almost.'

Dara was beginning to feel like she needed some familiarity in a foreign land.

'It's an English name too,' said Dara. 'I wonder if the owners are British, or even American.'

'Then let's go and find out,' said Ruben.

'What about if someone comes here looking for us?'

Ruben thought for a second. 'I'm sure they'll find us somehow,' he said.

Kreuzberg was quite different from where they were staying. There was a buzz about the place. Even if there weren't as many people as you'd get in Williamsburg, it had the same kind of vibe. Small bars with brick interior, vintage posters on the wall. Hipsters everywhere. They eventually found the Honey Pot. Upon opening the door, a little bell rang to announce their entrance.

'How quaint', said Dara looking around. 'Like an old-fashioned shop.'

A friendly mass of curly strawberry blond hair bounced across the room to greet them. The young woman who was evidently from England, showed them to a small round table in the corner. Dara sat down on the bench by the wall and Ruben sat on the chair. The woman went away for a moment and returned with a note pad.

'What are you having today?'

'You're English!' said Dara, evidently pleased.

'I am,' the young woman said with a smile. 'Now what can I get you?'

Dara smiled back, relieved to hear a familiar language. She might not have taken to someone like this in the States but now any contact was welcome.

'Two Americano's,' said Ruben, turning his head to speak to the young woman.

A young man came from the back of the cafe, wearing trendy jeans and a long-sleeved t-shirt with a pattern of an ape on it. He walked behind the bar and put on some music. Ruben thought it sounded familiar. He walked up to the bar.

'Who's this?' Ruben said, indicating towards the stereo.

'Blur,' the man said, his accent one of perfect Englishness.

There's no other way, there's no other way, all that you can do is watch them play'

Somehow Ruben thought the song sounded prophetic.

'So,' said the Englishman, leaning on the bar, 'I've not seen you here before. What brings you to our little cafe?'

'We just arrived in Berlin yesterday,' said Ruben. 'We thought we'd take a wander around the local area this afternoon. Do a bit of exploring.'

'Really?' said the man. 'Tourists? How long are you staying for?'

'It's complicated. We really don't know. Maybe a few weeks.'

'Any plans?'

'Not really,' said Ruben. 'It was all a bit last minute. What do you guys do around here?'

'Berlin is certainly known for its constant nightlife,' said the young man. 'We like to go to this local bar, not far from here. It's called *The White Russian*.' He pointed outside and Ruben could just make out a bar with a white sign further down the road as it curved around. 'It's more peaceful than some. Less techno music. It's called 'The White Russian' after its signature cocktail. We'll be there when we close up here at seven. If you want, we can show you the ropes, give you a few tips on what's what in Berlin.'

'That'd be great,' said Ruben. 'Like I said, we really have no idea about what to do here.'

The young man thrust his hand over the bar towards Ruben.

'The name's Justin by the way.'

Ruben shook the man's hand.

'Ruben,' he said. 'Good day to you, Justin.'

Ruben had an old-fashioned way of greeting people he liked which he thought sounded courteous.

Ruben thanked Justin for his invitation, and returned to Dara at the table.

'So, the guy I just spoke to, he mentioned that bar in the flyer we saw, 'The White Russian'. They drink there after work. He's invited us to join them later, when they finish up here.'

'Why did he do that?' said Dara, curiously. 'I mean, he doesn't know us from Adam.'

'Just friendly I guess.'

'I don't know, Ruben. Just seems strange to invite a couple of strangers to hang out with you. Don't they have their own friends?'

'You're reading too much into it, Dara. He seems genuine, just friendly. Maybe they don't have their own crowd here yet, after all they're foreigners just like us. It seems everyone here is from elsewhere.'

'I suppose,' said Dara. 'They do seem really nice. Pleasant. Kindred spirits. Anyway what else are we gonna do? We can always leave if we don't like it. They don't know where we live.'

Dara and Ruben spent a pleasant time chatting and drinking. As they were finishing up, Dara asked: 'Now where?'

'I thought we could go for a wander, see Potsdamer Platz, it's near,' remarked Ruben.

'Isn't it time to meet our new friends? Anyway, what makes the Potsdamer Platz so special?'

'It used to be a centre of social activity but it was flattened during the war. Then they put the wall in the middle of it. I wanted to have a look, see what's left. That's all. We've got time. It's only round the corner.'

As they got up to leave. Dara wondered what the point of visiting somewhere that no longer served as anything relevant but didn't say anything in case she was missing something. They said goodbye to the English couple, promising to return later to *The White Russian*.

When Dara and Ruben arrived at Potsdamer Platz, it was hard to imagine it had ever been anything other than a home for the modern glass skyscrapers, fashion chain stores and cafes that greeted them - the kind of building you'd find in any generic American city. Cars moved jerkily over the many roads of the intersection, getting in each other's way, frustrated at the absence of a clear path.

'This was once a hive of activity in the Weimar era, before it was divided in two after the Berlin Wall was erected. Not much of either could be seen now,' remarked Ruben.

The tall modern buildings dominated the skyline, almost obscuring the colourful pre-war history of the place. Whilst crossing the busy street onto a 'rest' place in the middle, Dara noticed a line of metal embedded in the ground, like a single tramline for a one-sided tram.

Dara hopped over the metal line and back again, one foot either side as people often do at the earth's equator, and then walked along it one foot following exactly the other, like a tightrope walker.

'It marks the old divide, where The Wall stood.' said Ruben, observing Dara playing along it like a child.

Dara imagined herself on the line thirty years ago, caught in the spotlight and shot at, and gave a shudder, causing her to return swiftly to the present.

A bit further up was the famous Brandenburg Gate,

'During partition, the gate was only partly visible from the West side,' Ruben explained to Dara, as if he was her personal tourist guide. 'The wall was placed right in front of it. There was even a viewing platform built for VIP tourists to take a look, a kind of watch tower on the West side. It's where J.F.K. stood on his visit, making sure the East side could see.'

'A gate opening onto an uncrossable wall,' said Dara.

Ruben nodded. 'Now it stands in the centre of the city,' he said, 'opening to the north, south, east and west. Mad to think this gate was once the entry point to the city, then overnight it was right in the middle.'

Ruben turned south from the Brandenburg Gate, walking at a brisk pace. Dara struggled to catch up. Half an hour later, the two of them found themselves standing in front of the Jewish Museum.

Ruben, said: 'This is what I want to visit, it's my reason for coming. Do we have time?'

'I don't think so.' said Dara. We've got to meet our new friends soon.'

'It's okay. I can come back again. I don't want to rush it. There will all be so much to take in.'

Ruben stood for a moment, gazing at the huge building.

'Come on, Ruben,' said Dara. 'our new friends will be waiting for us.'

CHAPTER SIX

Ruben and Dara were slightly late in their return. They walked quickly to the café, turning down a narrow street, seeing images of shop owners winding down for the day as they went past, clearing tables and stacking chairs to make room for the cleaners or returning unwanted clothes to the rail or folding them into neat squares and placing them purposefully back on shelves, ready for tomorrow's viewing, hoping the remaining customers would take the hint. A woman rustling around in the shop window moved mannequins around to their exact stage setting giving the appearance of life in her giant dolls house. A man moved boxes of fruit and veg from outside to inside, locking them up safe from the dangers of the night.

Dara and Ruben barely had time to register the fact that in this city, daily life shut down so early in the evening.

They quickened their pace.

Although this might have been the end of the working day, another life was about to begin, the baton merely being handed over, as bars were set, tables laid and doors opened, inviting in the Berlin nightlife.

When Dara and Ruben arrived at The Honey Pot, they found the owners had already shut up shop. The blinds were down and all was still.

'Oh, drat,' said Dara. 'Where was that bar again?'

Ruben looked up and down the street, putting his hand to his forehead as though it would make him see further but ended up looking like he was saluting to no one.

'It's around here somewhere. 'I think it's this way,' he said.

Dara double-checked on her phone and pulled Ruben down a different road.

The numerous bars that had their doors shut tight earlier in the day were now wide awake, full of dim light so as not to shine too brightly on its patron's souls or disturb too much the darkness of the night. It was early evening, and most of the bars were still waiting for their guests to appear, places laid in anticipation of their arrival.

Dara and Ruben looked momentarily through each window as they walked past in case they saw their new found friends sitting at a table, each taking a mental note of the interesting ones for another evening, if they fancied going elsewhere.

After walking a while, they ended back outside *The Honey Pot*.

'There it is!' said Ruben, pointing further down the road. 'I told you it was down here.'

'Let's go!' said Dara, before Ruben had the chance to rub it in her face.

The White Russian turned out to be only a few streets away from *The Honey Pot*. They walked through the wooden door into a dimly lit bar with exposed brick. This made it look like any bar in New York, but with less light and less chatter, a quieter atmosphere disturbed only by the scraping of a chair or clink of a glass. There weren't many people there at all. Ruben searched the tables and corners until he found Justin and the waitress from the cafe.

'Ah - you have come, I am so pleased,' said the waitress, now in civilian clothes.

'This is April,' said Justin, 'my wife,' and indicated for Dara and Justin, still standing uneasily, unsure if this couple were to be good friends or casual acquaintances, to sit. 'So happy to see you,' he added.

Ruben sat down and after a moment's hesitation, Dara followed and sat beside him. Both decided this was the right thing to do and became more at ease. A barman came over and placed four glasses in front of them. 'I took the liberty of ordering for you,' said Justin. '*White Russian* cocktails. Just the thing after a hard day's graft.' He pointed to the glass the barman had placed before Dara. 'This one has coffee in it, 'he said. 'They have fifteen different types.'

'It's very quiet in here,' mused Dara. 'Where is everybody.? What happens around here?'

'Ah... you really don't know Berlin do you,' answered April. 'This is pretty early for us Berliners. It may not get going for a while. We may get some people in looking for a quiet place after a night in a club.'

'*After* a club. But it's 6.30 - PM!' declared Dara.

'Yup,' answered April. 'That's the way it rolls in Berlin.'

The four young adults sat and chatted for an hour. About where they were from, about the music they liked, what life was like in America, what life was like in England, and a million other topics. It was clear they would get on. Dara loved hearing about April's life growing up in London and Ruben always had a fascination with the British public (private) school life which Justin experienced. A love of indie or alternative music gave them a central focal point and way to bond - the sort of music that crosses cultural boundaries by creating a universal, tribal culture, familiar to those in the know across the globe.

Gradually the bar began filling up with more and more people, but it still felt uncluttered. At least the buzz of new conversation gave it some atmosphere. Dara was fascinated by the people who came through. The way they dressed – familiar yet also different from their counterparts in Seattle, Atlanta or New York. Some styles seemed last year-ish yet some were totally unfamiliar and unseen.

The group had moved onto beers. Both Ruben and Dara had never experienced anything like the beer they were drinking. The first sip, Ruben thought he was in heaven.

'I've never experienced anything like this,' he said to Justin. It actually had flavour. A *Bud*, it wasn't. The next one he tried was different brand and taste again.

It was Ruben's round and so he walked up the bar.

'Vier bier, bitte,' said Ruben, pointing to the tap he wanted and marking every word so as not to get it wrong.

'Four Franziskaner,' answered the bar man. 'No problem.'

'Thanks, man,' said Ruben, suddenly sounding more American than he usually did.

He watched the man skilfully angle the tall, strangely shaped glass, narrow at the bottom, wide at the top, and the dark amber liquid emerged from the tap to fill each one.

Then something caught Ruben's attention momentarily - a short man behind the bar staring at him. Ruben looked back at the man, expecting him to avert his gaze, but the man continued as if transfixed. In the end, it was Ruben that averted his eyes, his attention drawn back to the task in hand of taking the four, now beer-filled glasses, back to the table. He gathered all the glasses together in his hands as quickly as possible, careful not to spill a single drop as he returned to the table. Sitting down, Ruben was constantly aware of the presence of the man's eyes having followed him like a painting in a spoof horror movie, though he did not mention it to anyone.

Ruben wondered if the little man was the owner, but soon found out this was not the case as the actual owner came to their table and sat with them.

'These are our new friends,' explained Justin. 'You know, the ones who've just come in, from America - the United States.'

'Ah, I see,' said the man, looking at them curiously. 'It is here.'

From the way Justin phrased their introduction and his subsequent reaction, it was as though the owner was expecting them. He had a strong accent, so referring to Dara and Ruben as 'it', though strange, could be explained away. English wasn't his first language, after all.

After a while, Ruben plucked up the courage to ask the owner where he was from and how he got here. The man, whose name was Maxim, did not keep his cards close to his chest, gladly telling Ruben his life story. Unsurprisingly it turned out he was, indeed, Russian.

'I came to East Germany in the early eighties,' he recounted. 'I come from a small village in Russia, so

Germany seemed like a much better option for an interesting life.'

Dara nodded in a slow measured way, fascinated at meeting a real Russian.

Maxim was tall with dark, slightly greasy hair, a moustache which seemed quite out of place at that time, and tanned skin. He looked like something out of a 70s menswear catalogue. There seemed something rustic about him, Ruben thought, rather than the military neatness and conformity he'd always imagined of someone typically Soviet Russian - all order and compliance. There was something old fashioned about him, combined with the ease of someone unorthodox. Maxim stayed and chatted for a while, then went away and sometime later returning with some free sambuca shots for the gang.

Ruben found it hard to focus or even stand up.

'I think we should go now,' he said, looking very green.

Dara, who was now chatting away to a couple of strangers, was reluctant.

'The problem is there's not the history in America like you have here....... buildings are new and -' Dara said to one of the strangers, before turning her attention to Ruben: 'Do we really have to go, the night's just getting started.'

'Dara, if I stay any longer, I'll fall on the floor. Do you really want to carry me home? Do you even know where we are?'

'All right then,' replied Dara reluctantly. 'And no I don't know where we are. I was hoping you would.'

'I dunno what's going on. I wish I hadn't drunk that last one.'

'Ask Justin for...'

'No no, we can do it. Let's just go outside and see what happens.'

'I suppose there's bound to be a cab or something.'

But then they got caught up in the music and the atmosphere in the bar and completely forgot what time it was. Within a short time, Ruben could barely stand and neither one of them had any idea how to get back to the apartment.

Too proud to ask his new friends, Ruben dragged Dara outside and they started walking up the road. But they didn't really know where they were going. After a while, they turned around and found their way back to the bar.

Then the short man who had been staring at Ruben earlier that evening appeared. He seemed to come out of the shadows, right on cue, as though this little piece of serendipity was scripted.

'Can I help you?' he said.

'What do you do for transport around here?' said Ruben.

'The U-Bahn runs throughout the night, or you could get a taxi,' replied the mysterious man.

'Yeh that would be preferable,' said Ruben. 'Do you have a number?'

'Where are you staying?' asked the man.

Ruben was about to answer, but Dara tapped him on the arm in an attempt to stop him. But it was too late. Ruben gave the stranger their address.

'How convenient,' said the man, 'I am going that way too. I'll order one.'

The man got out his phone and rang a number. Soon a car came and the pair had no choice but to accept the kindness of this stranger.

Back at the flat, Ruben and Dara lay on the bed, too weary to remove their clothes.

'I am glad to be back,' said Dara. 'Good call to go.'

'God that beer is strong,' replied Ruben. 'I thought I was going to hit the floor.'

The next morning, Dara and Ruben sat on the sofa, sipping strong coffee.

'What a strange man that Maxim is,' said Dara. 'He doesn't seem real.'

'Like something out of a movie,' said Ruben. 'People dress differently here. It's like everything's a mish mash of different cultures. We may not wear traditional national costumes but there are still small subtleties that mark our differences in the way we wear our global cultural uniform,' continued Ruben, desperately trying to avoid thinking about the little man behind the bar, who clearly wasn't supposed to be there.

'Do you think it's strange that the man came to help us?' asked Dara.

'Yes and no, I mean yes but I'm too tired to think about it so, no, I can't think about it now. Only that...'

'What, finish the sentence,' demanded Dara, now intrigued.

'I think I saw him at the bar.

'That makes sense, we were all at the bar.'

'Not *at* the bar,' replied Ruben with a yawn, 'He was *behind* the bar.'

Puzzled, Dara wanted to ask more about this seemingly insignificant incident but couldn't.

Ruben had fallen asleep.

When Ruben woke up, he and Dara decided to go back to *The Honey Pot* for breakfast. Dara remembered the breakfast menu, which included a 'full English' as well as 'American Pancakes'. Both of these sounded like the best thing to soak up yesterday's beer.

When they arrived, they were greeted warmly by April and Justin, though with some added concern. Justin left his place behind the bar and April stopped wiping down one of the tables, and they came over to greet their new friends.

'Hi, how are you?' said April

'We didn't know what had happened,' added Justin. 'Did you get home okay?'

'We thought we'd lost you. I'm so glad you came back,' said April.

'We found a cab,' said Ruben

'Actually a man called us a cab,' added Dara, almost feeling like it was a confession.

'The man behind the bar at *The White Russian* helped us,' said Ruben.

'Oh, really?' said Justin, surprised. 'What did he look like?'

'Middle aged. Short man. What little hair he had, shaved. And he had a wrinkled face.'

'He was wearing a hat outside,' said Dara

April breathed in deeply and was about to say something when Justin shot her a sharp look. April checked herself and smiled at the two new friends.

'Well, that was lucky,' she said. 'Glad you got home okay.'

'What are your plans?' said Justin. 'How long are you staying for?'

'We don't really know,' answered Dara. 'We came without any plan. Perhaps that was a mistake.'

'Oh, I wouldn't say that,' said April. 'There's lots to do around here. Opportunities too. What are you doing for money?'

'Actually we didn't think about that,' said Ruben, wondering if the money they had been given was supposed to be used for something particular. 'I guess I'll be looking for some freelance work. I'm a graphic designer. If you hear of anything . . .'

'We're looking for some help here now and again, if you're interested,' said Justin.

'We'll do it,' said Dara, shooting Ruben a look who she knew would be reluctant to take up a position he thought beneath him. 'When do we start?'

'Okay. I suppose,' agreed Ruben, reluctantly. 'I suppose we can work something out.'

'Come tomorrow and I'll show you the ropes,' said April.

After their breakfast, Dara and Ruben said goodbye to Justin and April. Dara was actually looking forward to working, gaining some sort of normality and routine in this peculiar situation, though the irony of leaving their job in a cafe to work in a café was not lost on them. Working in a cafe in Berlin, a place so foreign, did have a certain romanticism, Dara thought.

CHAPTER SEVEN

The following day, Dara made the morning coffee and thought about getting breakfast later at the cafe. The coffee machine was in a slightly different place than she previously remembered so she moved it back to its usual place, then left for the day. With a moment to himself Ruben was able to think more about the reasons he wanted to come to Berlin in the first place. As he reclined on the sofa, his feet resting on the coffee table, he heard someone practising the French horn nearby. He had a vague recollection that this wasn't the first time he'd heard it whilst they were here in Berlin, but he could place neither the time nor the tune. He racked his brain, Tchaikovsky perhaps. He put this question out of his mind for a moment, wanting to get back to focusing on his reasons for being in Berlin. Both he and Dara had almost forgotten the strange assignment that had brought them here.

The main reason for Ruben's interest in coming was to research his family connection to Berlin via his grandmother, and learn about her experience as a black woman during the treacherous times of the Second World War. What better way to research his Jewish connection with the Holocaust than from the very epicentre of Nazism? What a wonderful subject for a PhD thesis. But where to begin? The most logical place to start was the Staatsbibliothek - the Berlin State Library - just round the corner from Potsdamer Platz

Ruben went to the Staatsbibliothek via Checkpoint Charlie - once the main border crossing from East to West Berlin. Notorious for many successful, and unsuccessful, escape attempts, this single spot always held so much history and fascination for Ruben. When he got there, this monument to division had become a tourist attraction. You could even get a souvenir visa stamp to symbolise crossing the wall. The contrast to its previous life seemed trivial, yet harrowing at the same time. Where tourists in shorts gathered to have their photo taken, where people attempting to escape had been shot. Ruben wondered what the original border guards would have made of the scene.

Eventually Ruben reached the Staatsbibliothek, its 18th Century Neoclassical grandeur a stark contrast to the functional architecture of much of Berlin. Six Corinthian columns stood tall, their ornate leaf design holding up a triangle with Grecian figurines half-sculptured into the surface, their backs (or fronts) embedded into the surface, forever unable to move. The outside walls were pink which surprised Ruben. 'The thought of pink buildings conjured up images of Disney princess castles and Barbara Cartland, but somehow the Staatsbibliothek carried it off more tastefully. With the absence of anyone to talk to, Ruben's mind drifted to how the Disney fairy tales were based on traditional European children's tales, passed down aurally and gathered together by two German brothers. Further friezes on the face of the building were marked in squares along the walls, like 3D pictures, half bodies thrashing about, trying to break free, but suck in the mud, the three whole figures standing on top of the building the only ones to have found their freedom.

Ruben ascended the stairs to the entrance, feeling like he was entering the court of a Roman Emperor in a Hollywood movie, complete with lavish score. Once inside, he was greeted by the modern interior, neat, clean and functional, a visitors' desk made of plain chipboard, people in casual clothing milling about, rows of unremarkable shelves with mass produced books, concealing the more inspiring content. All was lit with fluorescent poles rather than goblets of fire, the grandeur coming from the sheer vastness of the space.

Walking around the many standard shelving units, Ruben felt dwarfed by the fact they didn't even come close to touching the ceiling. He didn't even know where to begin, and tried to look for a librarian who might help. Librarians were not easy to find as most people rocked the librarian look in Germany. He thought he spotted one, but when he approached the young woman, she ignored him and carried on scanning the shelves looking for the particular book she was after. Eventually, Ruben took a chance on someone else who happened to be the real deal, and she pointed him in the direction of the history section and World War II. But something was bugging him. That tune from this morning. He couldn't get it out of his head. It was so ingrained, he couldn't concentrate on looking at the array of books he had plucked from the shelves. He had to find out what that tune was.

Ruben found his way to the music section where you could listen to LP records. Being Berlin, there was a huge section of orchestral music. It was all very old school, but it seemed in Berlin there was a market for it. He gathered together all the Tchaikovsky symphonies, sat down on the slightly stained orange armchair by the record player next to the chair and put on the chunky leather headphones. Being a methodical sort, Ruben started with Symphony no. 1, carefully placing the black disk onto the record player. He moved the needle around to different parts of the record, jumping around to see if he could find the extract. It was a melancholic tune and slow and so deduced it must be a slow movement. He enjoyed reminding himself of the different bits anyway. Ruben didn't have long to wait to find his treasure. It was there, clear as day, the start of the slow movement of the Russian composer's second symphony. Satisfied with his prize, Ruben left the music section for the reading tables to study his books, failing to notice the man observing him and then immediately sitting down in the chair by the record player, checking out the records he had just listened to.

The man wore a pair of dark brown, dishevelled trousers, once smart but worn away by years of usefulness. His unshaven face and hairstyle which had long grown out, didn't help matters. The librarian noticed him more than Ruben, his scruffy appearance and furtive demeanour arousing her suspicions. She couldn't figure out what was amiss about him so said nothing, but kept a watchful eye. She watched Ruben too. Ruben piqued her interest - there weren't many like him in Berlin. He was kind of handsome too. She realised he was American but that only added to the intrigue. She followed Ruben to where he sat next, pretending to be busy putting books away.

She wanted to start a conversation to learn more about Ruben, so said in English: 'Do you need any further help?'

'Actually, I do. It's a difficult subject, especially for this country, but I'm researching the Holocaust. Have you got anything on the subject in English?'

'Yes sir, we have an English section. Come this way.'

The librarian led Ruben up some stairs to a floor that looked exactly like the floor below.

' Scheißer,' muttered the dishevelled man, discovering Ruben's disappearance. After a moment's hesitation he left his seat, and methodically started to look for his target in the rest of the library.

'We have this here and the one over here has had very good reviews,' the librarian told Ruben. 'These are well thought of as theoretical works on the subject.' The librarian continued, retrieving one of the books for the shelf in front of her. 'This one here gives a very personal viewpoint as it is based on numerous eye-witness statements. This one,' she said, getting down another book, 'is more academic and this,' handing yet another to Ruben, 'This one talks more about other minority groups who were also sent away, Gypsies, homosexuals and the sick. Oh, and this one is about the Black community that you asked for.'

Ruben took the books and sat down at a desk and started reading. The librarian hung around and was about to carry on with recommendations but as Ruben didn't continue engaging in conversation, she started to feel somewhat uncomfortable. She shuffled about a bit, before saying: 'I'll be downstairs, if you need any more help,' and returned to her post on the floor below. She passed the odd looking man from earlier on the stairs, watching as he stepped onto the floor where Ruben was sitting. She left it but she couldn't help wondering about this man who seemed more interested in the American guy than anything the library had to offer.

Ruben was fascinated to find a book on the history of black and mixed-race people in Germany during the war, the result of black French soldiers stationed in the Rhineland after World War I. He knew about the Jews from his father, but knew nothing of the lives of black people during this time. Ruben learned Hitler referred to them as Rheinland Bastards, and many were sterilised. Some were able to survive by performing in Vaudeville shows but many went to concentration camps. Ruben was extremely sobered by what he read, and the rare photos of an innocent looking schoolgirl alongside her classmates taken in Dachau brought a tear to his eye.

CHAPTER EIGHT

With the tourist bits taken care of in the first few days, Ruben and Dara settled into Berlin life as residents. They worked at *The Honey Pot* café, usually on alternate days to each other. Occasionally they did work at the same time during busy periods and at the weekends. Working in a cafe seemed to have more meaning or kudos than back home, and was much more fulfilling for both.

Dara and Ruben soon became like ships that passed in the night, each getting on with their day's work and coming together in the evening to sit on the sofa and watch films. Dara cooked when Ruben worked and most of the time when it was Ruben's turn to cook for Dara, he ordered take-out pizza. It was a pity, as Ruben was a good cook but he made such a fuss of cooking. He would usually make a grand gesture, some classic dish, usually French style, with all the ingredients and time and effort that entailed. Dara was content with making something simple, shoving something into the oven, making a salad.

Ruben loved doing the cooking at the café and even introduced a few new dishes including an all-American breakfast. He was finally able to put his creativity to use in a way that he was not able to that café back in the States. Justin and April seemed to be more up for employee input and invention. Dara liked the waitressing, taking people's orders, organising and making sure everything was in its place.

After beginning to discover Germany's black history in the books from the library, Ruben wanted to find out more. He thought about writing down the information he found, perhaps even making notes for a book. It would be something to work towards. The librarian was extremely helpful and found more photos and the very few articles written about the subject.

Dara meanwhile, on her days off, explored the city alone. She still had in the back of her mind their original mission, to find this package or document and bring it back to the gas station, even though Ruben seemed to have forgotten that's what they were here for. She wondered why they hadn't been contacted yet, though she was beginning to realise more and more that the writing on the saucer could be some kind of message. But what? And what was she supposed to do with it if they ever discovered what it meant? Perhaps wandering around the city was her way of trying to find clues in the absence of anything solid being presented to her. She couldn't help feeling she was missing something. She had the feeling the whole carousel, however inconsistent, seemed to be planned so she was sure something would happen soon. It was just a matter of waiting. A watched pot never boils, she thought, so in between her exploration of the city, she happily got on with her work washing pots in the café.

Some evenings were spent socialising. Mainly at what had become their local - *The White Russian*. Sometimes they went to gigs, usually at *Roadrunner's Paradise* on Saarbrucker Strasse. When Dara and Ruben first entered the place, they were gobsmacked. They'd never seen such a clean gig venue - a complete contrast to the usual dives bands played in the US. Here, the brickwork around the entrance was pristine, forming a pleasant courtyard, not the plastic open mouthed skull that marked the entrance to the *Vortex* in Atlanta. Justin and April liked their gigs and they went to see many of the English and American bands who played at the club. Ruben really got into *Fink* and Dara was thrilled to finally see PJ Harvey for the first time, having listened to her music at home. This seemed just like home apart from the odd band from mainland Europe like *Röyksopp*, which sounded unfamiliar with a strong electronic element, different from the guitar-based bands that dominated music in the States.

April and Dara went to PJ Harvey alone, without their significant others, though a few acquaintances of April's were there. They greeted Dara warmly and immediately. There didn't seem to be that judgmental aloofness Dara often found back home, and on occasion found doing herself. The clique mentality was so ingrained in the culture in the States, it didn't matter how 'alternative' you were, everyone was always checking you out to see if you were good enough to be part of their crowd – whatever they thought *that* was.

During the interval at the PJ Harvey gig, Dara went for a sneaky cigarette with one of April's friends in the smoking area. Their conversation felt natural and flowed like that of old friends. April's friend was German but spoke perfect English, and was fascinated by the differences between the English she was taught and the slightly different wording in American English.

'Nations divided by a common language,' she quoted, unable to disguise her thick and clipped German accent.

Fink always seemed to be playing. *Fink* were Ruben and Justin's favourite band, and they hung out drinking beers and listening intently to the music. It was a sanctuary for Ruben. Being able to actually listen to the band without the constant noise from the audience of rock venues he was used to. No loud Americans shouting at each other or getting into an argument for the sake of it, usually for some minor misdemeanour. Back home there was always someone shouting 'fuck you', threatening you in some other way or even starting a physical fight. Here in Berlin, everyone just watched the band, not each other, discussing life and music afterwards over another beer.

Some sort of trouble might start brewing outside in the *Roadrunner Paradise* courtyard late at night, but most of the time it was diffused by friends on each side before anything really happened.

One of Justin's friends said to Ruben at one of these gigs: 'There is not trouble here because we still can't get over being watched. Causing trouble had deeper consequences back in the DDR days. The Stasi had eyes everywhere.'

Going to gigs, going to bars, going to work – in a café. Their life was beginning to resemble that of their former life in Atlanta.

And still they waited for some sort of clue as to why they were in Berlin at all.

CHAPTER NINE

Dara was familiar with her role at the cafe, and had slipped into it with ease. At 7.30am she arrived for the early shift. She opened up the café, turned on the coffee machine and took the chairs off the tables and placed them on the floor. She put all the jars of cutlery on each table along with square wooden containers which held the condiments. Not long after she had done this, the pastries would arrive, which she carefully laid out behind the glass counter, like jewels in a display case. At 8am, the doors opened and people started wandering in on their way to work, picking up a croissant or Danish with their coffee, just like in New York, or Atlanta, or wherever people happened to be. Dara dropped each pastry sold - all made out of flour, butter and sugar, yet all completely different - into little white paper bags that didn't quite fit, leaving something beige poking out over the top as though trying to escape.

To make the coffee, Dara twisted knobs on the coffee machine and wedged the filter holder into its other half. Like a mad inventor's machine, it started to hiss and gurgle as if to show it was being industrious and producing the goods. On the odd occasion someone would ask for their croissant with cheese and ham, it had to be heated like a panini on iron grills which opened and closed like the jaws of a crocodile. These requests were so rare that it didn't warrant a second person quite so early and even Justin or April didn't appear until about 10am to open the kitchen - commuters being too busy for a cooked breakfast. She would then get on with the paperwork and bureaucracy of running a small business, and if Justin was in, he'd polish the coffee machine and countertop whilst chatting away to customers.

There were some who could afford the idea of a bohemian life where weekdays and weekends are one and the same, where the days go on indiscriminately, and these lucky individuals didn't emerge until noon.

At the coffee chain she once worked in, Dara didn't need to do table service but this was offered at *The Honey Pot*. Like her retail job at the thrift store, she interacted with customers, noticing their silent pleas for help, as they revised again what they were going to have for breakfast. A pain au chocolate became a cheese croissant, and a full English included maple pancakes, technically making it a hybrid American. However, Dara didn't begrudge these odd scenes which played out on the corner almost daily. They brought her out from behind the counter into the strange world of the stranger who, for a short duration, becomes an acquaintance or even a friend by putting their trust in you to deliver their order. Dara's lack of German didn't hinder her progress as most of the customers were British or international youngsters with a high command of the English language. When a young lady at a table having breakfast with a friend spoke to her one morning in genuine American style, Dara was pleasantly surprised.

'Eggs sunny side,' the young lady said. Her tone was natural but not quite harsh enough to be commanding even though it had a directness which was different to the polite requests from the other customers. Dara found this refreshing, or at least familiar.

'You American?' Dara asked the young lady.

'Half I suppose. My Dad is from Connecticut, and was posted over here with the military to the base in Bad Homburg. That's where he met my mom.'

The customer stopped the conversation short and looked at her companion. After this splurge of information, Dara was hoping the customer would continue, but by her quick cut off and focus on her friend, Dara felt dismissed.

'Well,' she said, 'let me know if there's anything else I can get you. Another coffee perhaps....'

But Dara may as well have been talking to the tables for all the notice the American and her friend took, so she returned to the counter. She felt a bit sad that her fellow

American was not more friendly. Dara was beginning to feel a bit homesick and so was disappointed at the rejection of the only thing that seemed familiar to her.

When the young American was paying her bill, however, she asked if Dara would be working the next day.

Dara could only muster up a one word answer: 'Yes,' she replied sheepishly, which was a little out of character for her.

'The name's Emilia,' the young American.

Dara wondered whether she would see Emilia again and why it was she wanted to know when she would be working in the cafe. Why not just swap numbers if she wanted to form a friendship? People sure did things differently here.

Back in the apartment, after a long morning of reading, Ruben decided it was time for lunch. He went out to a local food van for a sandwich and some chips. The man behind him in the queue seemed vaguely familiar but Ruben couldn't think why. So, with his sandwich in one hand, and a bag of chips in the other, Ruben headed back to the apartment.

When he arrived, Ruben found the main door to the apartment block unlocked. He walked up the many flights of stairs, not thinking too much of it, and put the key in the lock. He was sure he had locked both locks but apparently he had forgotten the main one that needed to be locked from the outside. He then sat on the sofa with his lunch, but had to get up again and pull the coffee table a little nearer so he could rest his feet on it.

After he'd eaten the sandwich and the chips, Ruben started to read but soon dozed off. In that moment between wake and sleep, he was sure he saw a shadow pass his closed eyes. He thought he also heard a slight creak and spontaneously half opened his eyelids. Perhaps it was all in the mind, a cloud or some creature overshadowing the sun for a moment but Ruben did wonder whether he should feel uneasy.

Later in the day, Dara returned from *The Honey Pot*, having finished her shift, and went straight to the kitchen with an unknown urgency.

'No 'hello' then,' remarked Ruben from the living room. 'What's so good about the kitchen? I'd have thought you'd have had enough of kitchens for one day.'

'Why d'ya move the coffee machine again, Ruben? I put it here to cover a mark on the surface.'

'I didn't move anything,' replied Ruben, coming into the kitchen.

He wasn't surprised at Dara's attitude. He was always in trouble these days. 'So what's with the obsession with coffee machines? Didn't you get your fix at work?'

The sound of the French horn start up, playing the now familiar tune.

'Not that again!' said Dara, slightly irritated.

'It's from Tchaikovsky's Second Symphony,' replied Ruben.

'You don't say? you always know everything.'

'I find out things, that's all. You should do the same.'

Dara suddenly got serious.

'Ruben, tell me, did you move the coffee machine?'

'No', Ruben replied, pissed off at her asking the same thing again. 'I did not move the coffee machine. What about you? Did you move the sofa?'

Dara grunted. 'What?'

'I had to move the sofa so I could put my feet on the coffee table earlier. That wasn't like that last night. It's been moved.'

'Well, it wasn't me,' snapped Dara and then repeated 'I didn't do it.' In a more concerned tone of voice, she added: 'What's going on, has someone been here? I mean we don't really know much about this place, do we?'

'Perhaps the place comes with a cleaner?' replied Ruben, almost sarcastically but not quite, as though he really did think they had maid service here.

'Yeah, right,' thought Dara out loud, not quite convinced something more serious was going on. An intruder leaving such obvious mistakes? Really? There was nothing to be done as there wasn't much evidence, but Dara had an idea.

The next day, after Ruben had left for *The Honey Pot*, Dara tied a piece of thread from the leg of the table in the hallway by the door and placed an umbrella on the other side. She then tied the other end of the thread around the umbrella, taut but not too tight. If anyone came in, they would disturb the thread without noticing.

Dara was the first to return. The thread was still standing. Dara almost felt disappointed. She was beginning to feel uneasy. They were clearly sent on a mission more than that of a simple courier but she had not considered that there may be other aspects to this than to retrieve the package and bring it back. Anyone coming into the flat must know they were out so they must be being watched. In addition to the horrifying fact that someone had been in their flat in the first place, and it seemed not for the purpose of robbery, it seemed likely both of them were being followed.

Ruben returned from his shift, and he too felt strange. He was sure one of the customers today was the same guy in the queue at the food van the day before. It was probably a coincidence. But then there was the American girl.

'Someone came in asking for you,' said Ruben, wondering how Dara had made friends with someone and not told him.

'Who?' She answered

'Emilia.'

'Oh, shit yes!' Dara had almost forgotten said she was working today. She really didn't think Emilia would turn up. People never do, do they? 'What'd she say?'

'Not a lot, just to meet her in *The White Russian* tonight for drinks.'

'And what did you say to that?'

'Nothing, just okay.'

'Did you get her number?'

'No,' answered Ruben indignantly. 'Why would I do that? Not if she didn't offer'.

'God you're useless,' she said.

'But she did leave this.' Ruben handed her a folded up piece of paper sealed with tape. 'I guess that's what you're looking for?'

Dara was getting impatient in Berlin, which was out of character and grabbed the note from Ruben. It did indeed contain what appeared to be a phone number.

Later, they sat down to dinner and ate in relative silence.

'Sorry,' Dara said, feeling bad for the way she'd reacted earlier, 'I'm on edge. Something's not right'.

'Yeah, I mean why would a complete stranger invite you out for a drink?' replied Ruben. 'Also this man came in, I'm sure I saw him when I was in the library and again in the queue at the food fan yesterday.'

'A bit obvious ain't it?'

'That's what I thought. Why would you show yourself so easily. Either he's not very good at it, or he wants me to see him.'

'Hiding in plain sight,' said Dara, casually trying to offer some kind of explanation.

'Another thing, April dropped a cup today. It was like she recognised someone. He'd been there a while but was kind of sitting with his back to the bar and somehow in the shadows. He was kind of nondescript, but I thought I recognised him. She was in an irritable mood all day after that.'

Dara thought for a moment. What could possibly be going on to have spooked April so badly?

CHAPTER TEN

Dara sat in the apartment looking at the digits on the folded piece of paper, wondering whether to ring it. April and Justin were great but sometimes it felt like they spoke a different language. It was sometimes hard to keep up. It would be nice to chat with a fellow American.

Eventually, she decided to ring the number and the familiar, slightly dismissive voice answered.

'Hello?'

'Hi,' said Dara, trying to sound enthusiastic. 'Is that Emilia?

'Yes, who is this,' came the short reply.

'It's Dara, from the Honey Pot, you gave your number to my partner, Ruben,'

'Ah, yeah, that's right.' Emilia's tone had changed to something more warm and friendly. 'Glad you phoned. Wanna go for a drink?

'Sure. *The White Russian*?'

'No, too noisy,' answered Emilia, almost aggressively. Dara really didn't have any other suggestions as she didn't really know anything other than the two places where her own life took place. *The Honey Pot* and *The White Russian*. 'We'll go to *White Trash*,' said Emilia, in such a matter-of-fact way, as if she was reading from a script. 'It's a bar, no 5 Schönhauser Allee. You'll like it, it's very American. How about tomorrow tonight. 8pm?'

Dara could do nothing else but say yes.

After saying goodbye to Emilia, Dara told Ruben about her 'girl's night out'.

'Fine,' said Ruben. Not wanting to be left out he continued: 'Perhaps I'll see what Justin is up to tomorrow night, then,'

'Whatever,' said Dara, not rising to anything Ruben might be directing her way.

Ruben texted Justin who immediately texted back: 'Usual place 8pm'

The following day was uneventful and would have gone unnoticed if it wasn't for the conspicuous absence of April at the Honey Pot. Justin was in with Dara. Neither really spoke much, though Justin did seem alarmed when she mentioned she was going to meet a fellow American for drinks - especially when she mentioned meeting her at *The Honey Pot*.

Dara tried to dig a little deeper: 'So what time is April coming in?' she asked, carefully watching Justin's reaction.

'I don't really know,' Justin replied, trying to be vague and hoping she'd drop the conversation, 'I don't think she's coming in today.'

Justin's vagueness gave him away. Surely he'd know April's every movement, thought Dara.

'What's she doing then?' Dara continued.

'Out and about, I think,' answered Justin.

'That sounds nice. Do you know where she went?'

Dara was beginning to irritate Justin, and she started to sense it. Justin brought the conversation to a halt.

'I really don't know,' he said, short and to the point.

Dara didn't know whether she was reading too much into his reaction, so put it out of her mind. She was more curious about meeting Emilia.

When Justin had finished what he had to do in the cafe, he left Dara to close up.

White Trash was an American Rock 'n' Roll bar. It had a timeless feel to it, with booths and vinyl covered benches that wouldn't look out of place in the 50s or in a familiar bar in Atlanta. There was a vintage Jukebox in the corner that played Elvis and Buddy Holly. Singers who had faded into obscurity, such as Chris Evans, were also brought back to life through the magic of the jukebox. Vintage guitars and posters advertising films and gigs of the day hung on the walls. *White Trash* wasn't a perfect replica of an American dive, this was Germany, but they did serve B52s frozen - something Dara had not seen for a while.

On entering the bar, Emilia greeted Dara with a smile, and they sat down at a small table. Shortly after, a waitress appeared.

'Hi there, how are you today?' said the waitress to Emilia with some familiarity, yet still keeping a distance. She was obviously German but had a slight American twinge to her accent, which felt reassuring to Dara.

'I'm good, thanks,' replied Emilia. We'll have two glasses of wine and some French Fries, loaded.'

'With Jalapeño's?' asked the waitress, anticipating the answer.

'I don't think so,' said Emilia, 'Hope you're good too.'

The waitress nodded. She didn't have time to go into a full answer as she had already taken the order. A tactic employed by Emilia, perhaps, Dara thought, so as to appear polite without actually having to listen to too much detail. Dara also noticed that Emilia hadn't asked her what she wanted to either eat or drink, just ordered for them both. But as Dara was happy with the choices made for her, she decided not to object, and the waitress left to get their order.

Emilia turned to Dara, her expression suddenly stern.

'What are you doing here?'

'It's a difficult one,' Dara replied.

'What brings you to Berlin?'

'It's a long story,' replied Dara, hoping Emilia wouldn't want the long version of the story.

But it was evident that she did.

'We've got all night,' said Emilia sitting back a little, indicating Dara should continue.

It wasn't that Dara didn't want to tell her. Emilia had a way of conveying that she could be a trustworthy friend and Dara really needed to tell *someone*, but at the same time she was hesitant because what she had to say sounded so stupid.

'We found an envelope,' said Dara. 'Inside was a note with instructions on something we had to do, and two plane tickets to Berlin.'

'Really?' said Emilia, intrigued, but not at all in disbelief, as though it was all this was perfectly normal in her world. 'Do go on, where did you find this envelope.'

'In the holder of a gas pump,' replied Dara timidly, as it did seem rather far-fetched.

'Right,' replied Emilia, trying hard to imagine the scene. 'So you just upped and left, no questions?'

'Yes.' It did seem rather stupid now Dara was hearing it out loud.

'What made you decide to come?' continued Emilia.

'Nothing better to do, I suppose.'

'Really?

'Well, you see, nothing was really happening in our lives. We were going through the same thing every day. Ruben, my boyfriend, was working at the same cafe he worked in as a student. I just worked in a shop. We were going nowhere. This was our chance. Something different. We would never have considered it otherwise. Actually it was Ruben who made the final decision. He's usually so cautious, I just thought, if he's up for it I should be too. So I suppose, yes, we just upped and left.'

Emilia listened intently to Dara's sudden confessional outpouring.

'Where are you living?' she asked.

'An apartment, near here actually. It was part of the deal. I bet you think we're really dumb to be doing this.'

'Not at all,' replied Emilia. 'Really I don't.' She could sense that there was something Dara wasn't telling her, but she planned to return to the subject later. 'So,' she said. 'How are you finding Berlin life?'

'Yeah, it's cool. Makes a change from the same old places in Atlanta. It's almost the same, though not quite. You've got such a mix of people here. It feels so exotic. I can find myself talking to someone in the cafe and it turns out they're from Finland or something. But I guess Europe is made up of lots of small countries as well as big ones. It's no different than finding out being in Atlanta and chatting to someone from San Diego, I guess. And they don't have elevators here. We're on the fifth floor. That's not great after a hard day at work.

'There are some quirks you have to get used to.' Emilia said. 'We are so spoiled in the States. So, where do you work, Dara?'

'A cafe, *The Honey Pot*,' Dara replied sheepishly. 'Myself and Ruben both work there.'

'Yes, of course.' Emelia berated herself for asking the obvious question, remembering it was at *The Honey Pot* they first met.

'It's only temporary, we're here to do something else.'

'What's that then?' asked Emilia, with less enthusiasm than before.

'We have to collect something, a package. We need to bring it back to the States.'

For the first time, Emilia looked alarmed. Dara assumed that it was because the idea of bringing back a 'package' which you don't know the contents of sounded like some kind of drug deal.

Dara justified herself: 'It's not what you think. It's papers, it's nothing bad. People do it all the time. My friend took some jewels across for some rich woman. It was easier to get someone than do it herself or have them sent by and impersonal courier like Fed Ex or something. It's like that.'

'I see,' said Emilia. Her curiosity had turned into suspicion - not of Dara - but the whole scenario. Any couriering of government papers from Germany, she would surely know about. She would remain calm and ask Ethan about it, see if he knew anything she'd missed. Not wanting to give the game away, she changed the subject to more conversational matters, as though she wasn't interested.

'So what's the apartment like?' she asked.

'Really nice, big, loads of light. There's someone who keeps practising a horn, though. The same tune over and over again. That can get annoying. I can't tell where it's coming from. The people downstairs aren't musicians and we're on the top floor. There doesn't seem to be anyone opposite. It's a real mystery.'

Emilia was about to say something, but stopped herself. Eventually, she said: 'Know anyone apart from the two Brits?'

'Not really,' replied Dara. 'Unless you count the Maxim who owns *The White Russian*?'

'Oh yeah, I know him,' said Emilia. 'I used to go there a lot.'

'Not anymore?'

'It got old,'

Dara continued: 'There was this one time early on in our stay. A little guy helped us get home when we'd had too much to drink. He got us a cab. Ruben had seen him earlier that evening behind the bar. He thought the man worked there. But he didn't. The strange thing was that Ruben said the man was staring at him, like he was trying to catch his eye, like they knew each other. After that night we never saw him again.'

Dara thought Emilia appeared a little agitated, before collecting herself.

The rest of the evening slid by with ease. Conversations about New York, LA, the Midwest and music, until it was time for Dara to go - explaining to Emilia she had to be up early for work.

As Dara left the bar and headed for home, she thought she saw Justin in the distance. Justin had his back to her and was talking on the phone. She was just about to say hello, when he slipped into an alleyway. It was evident he didn't want to be seen. But Dara was curious. As she walked nearer to the alleyway where Justin was hiding, she dashed inside a doorway next to the alleyway where she could hear him clearly without being seen.

'Kristof came into the café the other day. Thought I was in, but I wasn't. April saw him and got nervous. If she finds out what's going on, it's all over. Everything. We'll never get our hands on the telegram.'

So, the perfect couple were keeping secrets from each other, well Justin was anyway. Knew he was too good to be true. Poor April. Come to think of it she'd not heard from

April for a while. And what was this telegram he was talking about. Sounded important.

Justin continued: 'I'm going to get Ruben to come with me to London. Perfect decoy. That way April won't suspect anything or if she does, I can explain it away. She mustn't come with me to the gig. She'll see us for sure. The gig's sold out, so if I give my other ticket to Ruben there's nothing she can do about it. She'll be pissed off, but it'll pass. I may even say it's a lad's holiday. She can fuck off with Dara to Ibiza or the South of France, or something.'

Justin came out of the alleyway into the main street. The person he'd vaguely seen walking towards him hadn't passed and Justin found that odd, so he thought he'd investigate. Also, the person felt familiar but perhaps he was imagining things. He looked up and down the street, but couldn't see anything. Dara decided not to risk staying hidden and then being discovered if Justin walked past. She stepped out from the doorway as if it was the most natural thing in the world.

'Hello Justin,' she said. 'I thought I saw you there.'

Justin remained silent, and looked towards the doorway. He didn't need to ask why Dara had stopped in a random doorway. She volunteered the reason.

'Heel broken. All good now,' Dara said. 'See you tomorrow.'

Justin was left wondering if she had heard anything. If she had, she wasn't giving it away.

CHAPTER ELEVEN

By the time Justin reached Ruben at *The White Russian*, Ruben was about two beers in.

'Sorry mate,' Justin said, 'had to lock up and there were a couple of customers who took their time leaving.'

'No worries,' replied Ruben. Why were the British always saying 'sorry'? Justin was his boss. He had no need to apologise.

'Hope you didn't have to wait long,' continued Justin.

'Gave me a chance to have some alone time.

'Mmm…okay.'

Ruben thought to expand: 'Just sitting here people-watching, sitting with my own thoughts.'

Justin was none the wiser but didn't want to appear rude. He decided to probe again: 'So what do you think of, when you people watch?'

'Nothing much. This 'n' that. Wonder who they are, what they're doing here, where they've come from, where they're going. That sort of thing. Making up stories, really.'

'I guess I don't like making things up,' Justin said. 'I'm old fashioned, I suppose. My journalistic sensibilities mean I like to get to the truth, the heart of the matter. What is that person *really* doing and *why*. I don't sit in the corner and watch from afar, I go up to them and look them in the face and come right out with it. Not very British, is it?'

'Guess not,' replied Ruben, with a smile. 'More American.'

Justin smiled at that.

'You act more English than I do,' he said.

'Yeah, I'm very un-American, if you go for that cliche. I never used to be like that. I've become more old fashioned with age, though not old fashioned like you. If you see what I mean?' Ruben knew he was beginning to ramble, and should probably stop talking.

'I think I do know what you mean, Ruben. We both long for the way we imagine things used to be, but each from the opposite perspective. You're in search of the gentile America, long gone, swallowed up by vulgar ostentations that have now become the norm. 'Reality' housewives, rude and vacant, stupid and lazy. Not real housewives at all. They don't *run* the household, they live off their husband's earnings. Not saying there's anything wrong with that, it's just that they're *not real housewives*. Housewives *work*, even if they don't get paid. The way we used to live, it was so defined.'

'Oh those reality programs are so bad, that's not how most of us live.'

'Yeah I know, just wagging ya,' replied Justin. 'But it's not exactly the land of Tennessee Williams' gentlemen callers either, is it?'

'Not sure it was too much like that either, but yes there was a sense of calm and giving which seems to have evaporated,' said Ruben.

Justin continued: 'You see, me, the Brits, we're guarded. You can't get a straight answer from us. We never give ourselves away. You just get this vague politeness disguised as being friendly. It's unbearable. That's what I like about April. She is so moody half the time, you can always tell what she's thinking. Even if she doesn't come out and say it like I do. The British used to be much more direct. They didn't build bridges in the 19th Century by being polite.'

Ruben laughed: 'You're right. You built bridges. You built *connections*. We just get big business and takeovers. A quiet 9-5 may be boring, but at least it's stable.'

'Stability has never been my strong point,' replied Justin. 'Anyway, I've been meaning to ask, how did a boring square like you get a kick ass girl like Dara?'

'Hey,' replied Ruben pretending to be hurt. 'Opposites attract, I guess. She thinks I'm intellectual and classy.'

'You can fool some of the people some of the time,' replied Justin jokingly, slapping Ruben on the shoulder. 'Another pint?'

Ruben nodded vigorously.

'Two Francis Kahner's,' said Justin to the barman, hoping the beer would make up for his slightly challenging remarks, even if they weren't meant to be taken seriously.

'Here you go, mate,' said Justin, handing Ruben his pint.

'So what was that about "journalistic sensibilities" you mentioned,' asked Ruben. 'You a journalist?'

'Of a sort,' replied Justin. 'It's what I studied at LCC but you know, life gets in the way and now I run a café.'

'What's LCC,' asked Ruben

'The London College of Communications,' answered Justin before adding: 'Used to be The London College of Printing.'

'Sounds very practical,' remarked Ruben.

'It's in Elephant and Castle,' continued Justin.

'There's a place called 'Elephant and Castle'?' remarked Ruben.

'Yes, it's in London,' answered Justin. 'Pity you've never been to the UK, you'd fit right in. You should go sometime.'

'Actually, I've got some distant relatives in London. I keep meaning to go and visit. I was last there as a child, so don't remember much. Only that they lived in Notting Hill.'

'That's cool,' said Justin. 'Notting Hill is where they have the carnival. Bet your folks can see it from their window'

'I think they'd probably leave town whenever the carnival was on,' replied Ruben. 'I don't remember them as being much fun.'

It was time for Justin to come to the point, the real reason he wanted to hang with Ruben.

'April's had to go out of town. We'd planned a trip to London to see a gig, but we've had to change our plans. Why don't you come with me? You could catch-up with your relatives. You can have April's ticket to the gig. It'll be fun.'

Ruben didn't need much persuading after consuming three pints of German beer.

'I'll change the name on the Eurostar ticket and email it to you,' Justin said. 'You might as well have the gig ticket now.'

Justin opened his wallet and handed Ruben the ticket to the gig.

'Cardiac Arrest?' said Ruben.

'The Cardiacs, mad band, I'm sure you'll love it,' said Justin.

Back at the apartment, Dara and Ruben were out on the balcony drinking a nightcap, looking at the stars. Ruben mentioned his trip to London.

'You didn't think to ask me first?' said Dara.

'I didn't think you'd mind. I mean it was last minute.'

'What do you mean, 'last minute'?'

'The gig's in a couple of days.'

'A couple of days! You are leaving me here alone, without even bothering to ask me, and you're leaving in a couple of days!'

'Justin's got me a ticket to a gig. He's changing the name on the train ticket. I can't let him down now.'

Ruben got the gig ticket out of his wallet to show Dara. Dara snatched it out of his hand and threw it on the table.

'I overheard Justin tonight in the street. He was on the phone to someone, telling them he was going to get you to come to London. He said you were the perfect decoy. There's something going on that's for sure. And Justin is right in the middle of it.'

Ruben was stunned and didn't know what to say.

'What should I do?' he said nervously.

'Go, act as normal but keep your brain in gear. He said something about a telegram. It might have something to do with why we're here in Berlin. Oh, and I know of the band, you're in for a crazy ride. Not your sort of thing at all.'

Ruben nodded. He was really going to have to think on his feet.

CHAPTER TWELVE

Dara got a text from April the following morning as she was getting ready for work.

'Hi Dara, something's come up, too long to explain but in short, Justin and I need to take a trip to London. It means I can't be in today. Any chance Ruben could come in as well today? We really need you both to hold the fort. Sorry for short notice. Hope that's ok. Here's hoping – April.'

It was a familiar yet distant message, strange she didn't message Ruben directly but went through her instead. She wondered how to approach Ruben about it without making it seem weird that April had gone through a third party. Eventually the scene was set for her as Ruben asked:

'What's up babes? You look puzzled.'

Dara tried to sound casual: 'Just got a message from April. She said can you come in today as well. Something's come up. Neither of them can come in, so I could do with the help.'

'I was planning to go to the library,' replied Ruben. 'But I suppose it can wait.'

Both were feeling slightly uneasy about this sudden departure from the routine, and tried to cover up their apprehension with rational conversation. Things were getting weird but then, so was much of their recent life so they had become used to accepting anything out of the ordinary with a shrug of indifference. Ruben was beginning to worry even more about April. He hadn't seen her since the day she evidently recognised the strange man in the cafe. Until the text from April just now, there had been no communication from her at all.

Whilst mildly annoyed at having to go in on his day off, Ruben was also relieved as he was beginning to feel even more uneasy than he usually did - especially now the trip to London appeared to be something more than he first thought - and was pleased to be in sight of Dara for the day.

Both went in together, even though it really only needed one of them to open up and set up for the day, the second person - usually April or Justin - coming in for busier periods. Dara and Ruben sought comfort and solidarity in their partnership. With the two of them there was no rush and the day passed uneventfully. It was unusually quiet at *The Honey Pot* that day. Just a few dribs and drabs. Not much cooking to be done.

A lone twenty-something female came in and sat reading for some time. She was in her own world, seemingly unaware of her surroundings. Eventually she left and it was like she had never been, leaving no mark or impression on the place, or Dara and Ruben. A French couple ordered black coffees and cut through the thick silence with their constant bickering in a language neither Dara nor Ruben could understand. When the bickering couple left, the foggy silence filled the room once more, each sound amplified: the whirl of the heating, the clink of a cup being laid down on a saucer, a bird screeching heard as clearly within the walls of the cafe as if there were no walls at all. One guy dared to ask for food and Ruben found himself cooking a full English, the only meal of the day. Echoes from the kitchen of sizzling sausages, clunking pans and hissing water and cooking oil filtered through to the main dining room.

Towards the end of the day Ruben was in the back clearing out the trash. Dara was putting the chairs on the tables, humming to herself. Suddenly, from out of the shadows, April appeared. Dara jumped and gasped, catching her breath.

'What the hell! What are you doing here?' she said anxiously, though she didn't know whether she should actually be relieved to see her friend after the unexplained absence. April was standing in the doorway behind the bar that led to the cellar, out of view from anyone looking through the windows from the street.

'Shhh! No one must know I am here. It's too dangerous. I - me and Justin - need to lay low for a while. We're going home. You must keep a low profile too. They're beginning to suspect. They're even onto you guys but they don't know, not really. They haven't got any evidence. But it's not safe for us here at the moment,'

'What do you mean, they're *onto* us?' said Dara, then calling out to the kitchen, 'Ruben, come out here. It's April.'

'They're following you both,' continued April. I wasn't sure if they would do anything, especially as they've got nothing on you.'

'What the fuck? April, you sound insane. What the hell are you going on about? Ruben!'

'You need to listen. It's why you're here. You must know that by now. What you are after - the thing you have come to collect - everybody wants to get their hands on it. If these guys think you have it, they'll do something bad for sure. You are both in danger.'

'What the hell are you talking about?' whispered Dara. 'You're making me scared. If we are in danger then do something about it!'

'I'm trying. I need to get Ruben out of here. They seem to be tailing him closely now. Even if it's just to send them in the wrong direction.'

'What does that mean?' replied Dara getting even more agitated. 'Ruben!'

April calmly answered: 'I had to do something quickly, I've been laying low watching them watching Ruben. They aren't so secretive; their intentions are clear. And they'll do anything to get the slightest bit of information.'

Dara rushed out to the kitchen.

Ruben was gone.

She put her hand to her mouth, tears filling her eyes, and yelled at April from where she stood.

'April, where's Ruben?'

'You need to stay calm,' answered April, coming into the kitchen area and looking sharply at Dara. 'We need to pretend everything is normal, that we don't know they are watching any of us. That's why you need to stay here and act like nothing's happening. You are just going about your usual routine.'

'What about Ruben?'

'Ruben is fine, I've sorted it,' answered April.

Dara was getting increasingly frustrated with April taking her time to tell her where Ruben was.

'Will you please just tell me where he is!'

'Keep your voice down,' whispered April. 'Someone might hear. I've just seen Ruben outside and given him a Eurostar ticket to London leaving in an hour. He can't go to London with Justin as they'll follow them, it's too suspicious. He needed to leave right away so as not to give them a chance to follow him. He couldn't come back and say goodbye as they would see that and know something was up. I'm hoping they won't notice for now. But if they do, Ruben won't be leading them anywhere apart from on a wild goose chase. He mentioned he had relatives in London and so that's where he's headed. If they follow him, they won't find anything there. It's a red herring.'

'My god, April! What is this? What have you got us into?'

But Dara found herself talking to the open door. April was gone. Like Princess Leia's hologram switching herself off after relaying an important message.

CHAPTER THIRTEEN

Ruben had gone casually into the back yard, dragging two bin liners containing a rainbow of rubbish to the bins. As he dragged the bags down the small step and onto the concrete ground outside, one of the bags split.

'Damn you trash,' he muttered, and started to gather up the different coloured peelings, unwanted food, coffee grinds and unused paper napkins. Out of the corner of his eye he noticed a shadow standing over him. He looked up.

'April! What are you doing here?'

He was expecting some kind of joking remark, but April seemed different. Something wasn't right.

'Ruben, you need to listen. This is serious,' she said.

'Okay,' said Ruben, jumping to attention at this command.

'You need to go. You need to go now.'

'What? Why?'

'I have no time to explain in full but you are being watched, we all are. But I think you know that. You are in serious danger.'

Ruben's demeanour changed instantly. 'Okay,' he said. 'What do you want me to do?'

'I have a new Eurostar ticket for London. It leaves tonight. You mentioned you had relatives there. Go to them, or stay in a hotel, go sight-seeing. Do anything you want, just don't go with Justin or you'll lead them to our agents. If you go now, there's a chance they'll not notice. You need to be out of the way for a while. You can't have anything to do with the reason why you came here, or with us. You are our diversion.'

'What about Dara?'

'Keep your voice down,' hissed April. 'She'll be fine, I'll look after her. We need to make sure the rest of us are carrying on as normal so they don't suspect anything. Dara needs to be here as though nothing is going on. You're just going on "vacation", as you say over in the states. It can't lead them to anything.

April handed Ruben a Eurostar ticket and his passport.

'How...?' began Ruben.

'There's no time,' said April. 'Go!'

And Ruben bolted out of the yard, leaving the bags behind, and headed for Berlin Central Station and got on a train bound for Paris.

Some hours later, Ruben arrived at Gare d'Est, in Paris.

He ran, down the escalators, through the turnstile and onto the metro platform. It was only one stop but thought this the quickest way, and the best way to get lost amongst the crowd on the underground. He was acutely aware that he was being followed still. However fast he ran, he could not escape the eyes and ears of his pursuers who seemed ever present without a flinch of panic. The platform was not long and there was no train conveniently waiting to jump on just before the doors closed, just before the hunters got there, leaving them gawping at their prey as he gently sailed off into the distance. There was an opening at the other end of the platform with stairs going upwards just visible, poking out of the black hole marked only by an 'exit' sign on the wall above, so he ran towards it. Just then, a train rumbled into existence and came to a screeching halt. In a split decision Ruben thought NOT to get on it but continue up the staircase which was increasing in visibility, the more he ran at the other end of the platform. He ran through the darkness out of sight. The men chasing him got to the platform in time for the train and assumed he was on it, so jumped on.

It was a new train with no door partitioning off each carriage. The pursuers smiled with delight. They had him now. Getting on the last carriage, confident in their success, they started to move slowly down the aisle, steadying themselves on each intersection like a concertina, with no hand rails and a revolving floor. But they got to the end and found themselves empty handed.

Meanwhile, Ruben followed the stairs up and ran through the station foyer. Seeing another set of stairs with the glimmer shining through, he headed straight for them and to his surprise found that they lead right onto the street. With no barriers on the Paris Metro, unlike New York, to force a pause and slow him down, Rubin found himself unexpectedly on the street gazing at the daylight, slightly confused. He watched the people walking across the street, down the steps to the metro, some struggling to carry heavy shopping plastic bags and wicker baskets. Others casual with hands in their pockets, skipping down the stairs, looking forward to their destination. He observed the tall 19th Century apartment blocks, seen only in photos before and thought for a moment he was a tourist, before an apple tumbled out of someone's basket onto the floor in front of him, bringing him back to the present. Ruben gathered himself and continued to flee. He ran down a side street and stopped to check the direction before continuing, this time perused by time. Out onto a grand boulevard and finally to the big glass doors of the Gard du Nord. Ruben found himself in the vast space. Busy with people coming in and out, the glass doors barely had time to shut before sliding open again for people who had a purpose, leaving to go home. Those entering knew their place, which platform to go to for their train out of there. There were pockets of chaos too, tourists stopping in mid space to stare incomprehensibly at signs, disturbing the people heading straight for their destination as they tutted and walked around them reluctantly. Ruben was one of these, staring at the tracks and trains directly in front of him. The boards above showed the city destinations and times. Looking intensely, he couldn't see London but a jolt to the right arm from a would-be passenger caused him to spin his head to the left where he saw the Eurostar sign and trains to London.

Ruben composed himself on the outside. He did not want to draw any unnecessary attention to himself. Inside he was breathing deeply, he had to get this train, as though all would be well if he did. His eyes followed the direction of the sign, high above his head, parallel with the top of a pair of very tall escalators both moving upwards. His gaze followed the escalator down to the bottom where it met the platform. The counter movement made him giddy but with his eyes on the prize he walked to the starting line with a slight stagger and gingerly stepped on the ride, floating upwards in a moment of tranquillity. Reality hit, as at the top of the escalators the remnants of a queue still remained, muttering as though one entity. The guards were ushering people through security and customs in an attempt to get them through in time to catch the train that was about to leave but Ruben was still forced to pause.

He always hated being late, and this was really cutting it fine. He was on his own and didn't have Dara to pull him up. He'd had no time to think about how much he hated the diabolical situation he found himself in. He was not one to run, whether to catch a train or run away from someone. The situation occurred so suddenly he had no time to think and could only take the orders from April without a moment's consideration as to whether it was the right thing to do.

'Bonjour, ello,' said the security guard, unflustered, bringing Ruben back into the room, as he ushered Ruben through. Ticket scanned and passport checked, he entered the departure lounge. People were huddled in different queues near the exit to the platform which marked their section of the train suitcases.

An attendant was helping people onto the train and storing their luggage.

'Your bags sir?' he said to Ruben. 'Can I take them?' The attendant looked confused and a little embarrassed when Ruben told him there was nothing to take. This made Ruben suddenly feel conspicuous as he was sure his lack of any luggage would draw more attention to him than the holiday makers who did not care to travel light.

Once on board, Ruben moved along the aisle hurriedly hoping the attendant had instantly forgotten him. He moved along in a methodical fashion to seat number 25A (as indicated on his ticket) only to find there was someone sitting there. Ruben didn't want to draw yet more attention to himself so he moved on down trying to emit an air of nonchalance, in order to figure out what to do when reaching the gap in the carriages. He sat down on the folding seat there. Looking at his ticket he saw that it wasn't his carriage, something the attendant had not picked up on in the confusion, so he cautiously moved from one to the other and found his seat. If the men following him were on this train, there would be very little any of them could do about it, as all would be trapped on the train with no means of escape, tied to their seat number.

Ruben began to breathe again. He grabbed a magazine from the rack in front of him in an attempt to look like a seasoned traveller. He was in a near state of relaxation, but still with the awareness that all was not necessarily over. He took the opportunity to close his eyes for a moment and lay his head back on the headrest. It had been a long day. He slept lightly, wondering what on earth any of this was about.

What seemed only seconds later, Ruben heard the train hostess approaching with a trolly packed with goodies. He ordered a mini bottle of red wine. The woman was smartly dressed, like an air hostess, the picture familiar to anyone who flew often from city to city back home. It was strange to see a hostess on a train - just one more oddity since landing in Berlin.

'Mushroom or beef?' came her soft but matter of fact voice. Ruben looked confused so she continued. 'Are you a vegetarian?'

'Not today,' muttered Ruben.

The train hostess pulled down the seat tray from the back of the seat in front of Ruben, picked up a plastic tray of food from inside the narrow trolly, and almost flung it into his hands. She then untwisted the top of a mini bottle of red wine and plonked it on the tray. Without lingering, she moved on up the aisle, Ruben hearing her repeating the conversation she had with him almost in its entirety with the next passenger, until the entire carriage had been subjected to her brisk style of customer service.

The food wasn't too bad, though like the wine, it was in miniature. Slices of beef with potato salad. A slice of French baguette. A small yogurt, a small plastic cup of water and the miniature bottle of wine.

After Ruben had eaten, he must have dozed off but instinct woke him and he saw a familiar man enter his carriage. The man looked at Ruben with a menacing glare as if to say, *We've got you, there's no escaping us now*. The man then turned around and walked back through the carriages to where he came from.

Ruben needed another plan.

CHAPTER FOURTEEN

Ruben wondered what he should do when he got to London St Pancras. Should he just run or should he wait? If he did run, where would he run to? And if he waited, what was it should he be waiting for? The fact he knew his pursuers were on the train made either plan fraught with danger. The difficulty was that he had no knowledge of London St. Pancras whatsoever in terms of what he would find there to use as a defence, where any of the exits were or even where they would exit to. He was still hungry, and needed something more than wine. He went to the buffet car to get a coffee and some 'crisps', as they called them in the UK. The buffet car was one carriage further up the train - therefore in the opposite direction from where the men were. As he made his way along the aisle, Ruben noticed a plastic bin liner filled with trash was by the door just before the buffet car. At that moment, the train rolled to a stop, and an announcement came over the tannoy.

'International. The train is not scheduled to stop here. Please do not leave the train.'

The door opened and one of the buffet staff got off. Without thinking, Ruben followed, taking a chance the staff member would not notice or be bothered. Ruben was right. The staff member looked around at him, and shrugged. It had been a long day, and whatever this passenger was up to was no concern of hers.

Off the train and finally out of danger, Ruben could take a moment. He stood on the desolate platform of the nondescript station. He was completely alone. The platform seemed to serve domestic trains as well as the Eurostar and one came through and stopped for a moment to let a few people off. They strolled, heads down with their work bags, briefcases, tool bags and some with tote bags, laptops sticking out of the top - unaware of danger.

According to the sign on the platform, Ruben saw that he was at Ashford Station. Not knowing the lay of the land, his cautious nature took over and he decided not to jump on wherever the next train was going. It was tempting to keep moving. But too risky. The train may lead him into the hands of his pursuers, or an even worse fate. He examined the timetable contained within large plastic frames on a stand, set out like a book but on hinges so you had to move each heavy page to see the next. Standing in between the pages hid most of Ruben from view, only the bottom part of his legs and feet in view. He was conscious, however, that if he stayed here too long it would eventually cause anyone looking at the CCTV to become suspicious, so after a brief study of the names of some of the stops on the line, he headed towards the bathroom. Here, he was out of the way. Hidden to a certain extent he looked up the various towns he could remember on his phone. He didn't want to stay too long so he wandered out again and while he considered his next destination, ordered a coffee and a small square cake at a little café perched on the platform.

Ruben noticed that the next Eurostar stopped at Ashford, this time a scheduled stop. He considered waiting for that and getting on, hopefully unnoticed, but thought better of it. It was highly likely that realising they had lost him on the last train, they would be there waiting for him to get off the next. There were four more Eurostar trains today, and when it was realised Ruben wasn't on any of them, his pursuers would conclude he had probably got off here at Ashford, sending them in his direction. It was a long shot that they would think of this but there was still a risk. He thought about catching a domestic train to another London station but his linear train of thought advised otherwise. The next train to arrive was to the seaside town of Margate, so Ruben took that one.

There were a few people scattered about the carriage, some in groups, all seemingly isolated from each other. A mother struggled to keep her two small children seated as they ran around the carriage. 'Shell, sit down, we'll get an ice cream when we get there.......Marlon, stop hitting your sister.......' She wanted to extend her ticket to Margate. At least they might calm down a bit then. A teenage couple were necking, barely pausing for breath even when the ticket inspector came over. The youth handed him the tickets without a moment's rest. The inspector muttered something about getting the slow train via Ramsgate, and so they got off at the next stop at Canterbury West.

Two youths in cheap branded clothing got on at Canterbury West and started advising each other about the mysteries of bra straps, before turning to the subject of football: 'Arteta's really got to change the way he sets up the team without Aubameyang.'

'If we do get through Chelsea's defence, without him there's no-one to bang em' in.'

I'd rather we score this afternoon than I score with Cazza tonight. That's how much I hate Chelsea...'

… and so it went on.

After careful thought, Ruben convinced himself that no-one in the carriage were part of anything.

'Tickets please,' said the ticket inspector. Ruben wondered what to do. He didn't have long to think as the inspector was standing over him, carrying some sort of metal machine and didn't appear to be going away.

'I lost it,' he said, somewhat clumsily. 'I didn't have time to get one.'

The ticket inspector sighed, rolling his eyes and casually said: 'American, are you?'

Ruben nodded, almost ashamed.

'Listen,' said the ticket inspector, 'you are supposed to purchase tickets before boarding. You're not allowed to travel without purchasing a ticket.'

'Can I get one now?' asked Ruben sheepishly, expecting to be arrested or at least thrown off the train.

'I suppose so,' sighed the ticket inspector. 'I'm not supposed to do this, you know.' He swung round a larger metal machine that was over his shoulder as if it were a bag. 'Where are you going, sir?'

Ruben thought for a moment. He really didn't know. 'The end of the line?' It was more of a question than a statement, and he wasn't really expecting an answer.

'So that's a single to Margate then, sir,' said the inspector. 'Are you travelling back today?'

'I don't know. Probably not.'

'Are you travelling back within the next three days, sir,' continued the inspector. 'And will you travel after 9.30 in the morning?'

'I don't know,' replied Ruben, getting a little irritated at all these questions. Was this ticket inspector really an imposter trying to gain information from him?

The ticket inspector sighed: 'I'm just trying to ascertain whether I am to give you a cheap day return, an off-peak saver return or an open return. Are you planning on returning at all, sir?'

'Actually, at this stage, I just don't know. I really don't know what I'm doing.'

'So that's a single ticket one way to Margate then,' concluded the inspector, keen to move on. He typed something onto the keys on his machine which caused it to ring, and then make a whizzing sound before spewing out a ticket.

Ruben handed over his credit card and input his pin into yet another machine attached to the inspector. The inspector gave a nod before moving on to the next set of seats. Ruben sat back and relaxed. He heard the machine ring and whizz again (apparently the whoever's ticket that was wasn't going far enough), and the next one was the wrong kind. All in all, no one on the carriage had managed to purchase the correct ticket.

Ruben wondered if all England was this chaotic.

Alone in a corner of the carriage, sat a man. Ruben fixated on him. What if he had been followed? What if this man was one of them? What if had a knife or a gun? Ruben never found out as the man got off at Ramsgate.

The train eventually pulled into Margate station, slowing down before grinding to a halt. Ruben disembarked from the train. Being a seaside town, the screeching of gulls provided a constant soundtrack that could not be turned off. One gull had got into the station and was not afraid to fly next to Ruben's head, flapping its wings loudly to menace a potential victim. Realising he didn't have any food, the gull swooped off, out of the station and into the sky beyond.

The gull's ravenous attitude reminded Ruben of his own hunger, something that had slipped his mind in the drama. He had not eaten for some time and so left the station as quick as he could, and followed the signs to the seafront to see what he could find. Having grown up in California with the buzz of life on every inch of the ocean front, the seafront at Margate was certainly a culture shock. Everything seemed shabby and closed, though on closer inspection the various shops selling postcards and sticks of rock were actually open, they just didn't seem it. There was no blaring music or colourful characters to welcome anyone into any of these places. Ruben couldn't see anything that stood out in terms of a place he would like to eat in. None of the tired looking restaurants or food shacks took his fancy. And the places claiming to be hotels looked more like empty houses.

Rubin soon found a greasy spoon cafe to his liking, selling fish and chips. He'd heard about fish and chips as something quintessentially English and thought now was as good a time as any to try. One set of chairs and table was placed outside in an attempt to look summery and festive, but they were lonely and unused as the cold bit through the town.

Inside, the cafe was decorated with little effort or thought to aesthetics, inhabited by cheap plastic chairs and Formica tables, once white but now with a grey tinge. Minute lines were scratched into the tables, colourfully stained with anonymous, irremovable food stuff.

Ruben sat down at the first table inside the door. A waiter came over and gave Ruben a plastic three-fold menu. He waited a while without saying anything while Ruben tried to make sense of the different sections. Aware of the man staring down at him, Ruben looked up.

'Give me a moment, please,' he said.

The man interrupted him and started reeling off a list of changes to the menu.

'The sausages are not the usual brand of Cumberland, they're from a different supplier,' he started as though Ruben was a regular, and actually knew what a Cumberland sausage was.

He continued: 'No plaice today, but we do have skate as a special. Just to say we do have Heinz at the moment, not any of that Blackwell rubbish.'

'Heinz what?' asked Ruben.

The waiter looked shocked. 'Baked beans of course,' he replied.

With this new information, Ruben studied the menu in further detail and pretended to consider all the options the waiter had presented. In reality, he was confused about many of the combinations but was aware of the waiter's presence and that it was clear he was not going to go until he'd decided what to have. Slightly anxious about being watched, Ruben skimmed the fish section and ordered the first thing on the menu.

'I'll have cod and chips,' he said.

'Right you are,' replied the waiter. 'Mushy peas?'

'What,' replied Ruben slightly horrified at what he thought he heard. Had the waiter just called him "mushy"'?

'Would you like mushy peas with your cod 'n' chips, sir? 50 pence extra.'

'Fine', replied Ruben for the sake of argument and so the man would just stop.

When the huge fish in batter arrived, Ruben realised it was an acquired taste - greasy and crunchy with soft flaky bland white fish inside. But it tasted so good after his overwhelming day. The chips were not like the slim French fries of home but thick and chunky. Like the fish, they managed to be soggy and crunchy at the same time. He saw other people add vinegar and tried the same. This took away any crunchiness the chips had but it did give everything a sour taste which cut through the grease. There was some green gunge in a ramekin on the plate. At first Ruben thought it was guacamole, an unusual dip for potato fries. After dipping in a chip in the green gunge, he realised it was the mushy peas.

'Oh, peas that are mashed,' he said to himself out loud - an absolute revelation.

There were many jars on the table too. The usual tomato ketchup, an unusual brown version and tartar sauce.

Despite the grease, the fat, the deep-fried batter, potatoes and questionable vegetables, the meal sat contentedly in Ruben's empty stomach. Finishing off what was left on his plate, there being no sign of the waiter, he got up and went to the counter to pay.

The waiter came out from the back room and rang the till.

'That'll be £5.50,' he said.

Ruben got out his credit card.

'£10 minimum,' said the waiter.

'What?'

'We only accept cards over £10, sir. Do you have cash?'

We've got some brown sauce for sale. And some white vinegar. We can make it up to £10.80 with two of each,' said the waiter, happy he'd found a solution.

Ruben was bemused, having no idea what he'd do with four bottles of condiments, but went along with it and handed over the card.

'There you go,' said the waiter, handing over a thin white plastic bag with the sauce bottle and the vinegar. With that, Ruben left the cafe and found himself outside on the street with his carrier bag of bottles.

Ruben really needed to sleep. But where on earth would he begin? He walked along the seafront looking at the large terraced buildings that overlooked the sea. They all had bay windows with white stucco columns leading up to the door, paint peeling off like the scales of a fish. Ruben tried to look through the windows to gain some sense of the places he passed in terms of spending the night. Most of the windows were so grubby, it was difficult to see through to the inside.

One window was more welcoming with a standing lamp illuminating the room behind it. A cosy room with an armchair in the corner, a bookshelf beside it with only a few books, but books nonetheless, a TV flickering calmly and a moving hostess trolly with a pot of tea and plate of biscuits. The person pushing the trolly was just out of view but Ruben wanted so much to be sat in that armchair, watching the TV with a hot drink. He marched up to the front door and rang the bell.

Even though it was billed as a hotel, the place looked so much more like a cosy home it didn't seem right to just walk in. An older woman opened the door. She had short grey hair, curled in the Marilyn Monro style. Once a symbol of young independence, it now suggested a woman of a certain age. She wore a smock over her nylon dress and Ruben could just make out the pattern of pink flowers outlined in brown.

'Hello there,' she said in a soft, kind voice.

She didn't say any more so Ruben continued for her.

'I'm looking for a room for the night,' he said, as politely as possible. 'I don't suppose you have one available?'

'I do, as a matter of fact. Room number 7 – lucky for some,' she replied cheerily. 'My name is Louisa.'

'I certainly hope so,' said Ruben with a smile. 'I'm Ruben.'

'Well, come on in, Ruben. I've just made a pot of tea. I'm watching Coronation Street.'

Ruben had no idea what that was, but anything was good right now, so he followed Louisa inside, into the front room and sat down in the armchair, happy to be now part of the picture through the window.

'Do you not have any overnight bags?' asked Lou. Seeing Ruben was a bit agitated and lost for words trying to find an excuse, she continued, saying gently: 'You don't have to answer that.'

'What have you got in that bag,' Louisa said, pointing to the white plastic bag containing the bottles from the chip shop.

'I was in the café down the road and I had to pay £10 by card as that was their minimum. You can have them if you like.'

'Do you mean 'The Fish n Ships' a few streets down?

'Yes,' said Ruben for the sake of the conversation as he realised in his haste for food, he hadn't actually looked at the name of the place.

Ruben had started to doze off. Louisa showed him to his room.

'Here you go,' said Louisa, handing him a key with a large plastic attachment with a number seven on it. 'It's the first floor to the left. The bathroom's to the right, and breakfast is any time from six-thirty.'

'Breakfast?' said Ruben.

'It's included in the price. And thanks for the brown sauce, it'll come in handy in the morning.'

Ruben was delighted the full English came with the room so he wouldn't have to go looking for more food tomorrow in such a strange and uninviting place.

In the dining room, early next morning, the basics were laid out: the familiar brand of Kellogg's Corn Flakes, plus some unfamiliar brands of different cereals, and one called *Alpen* that sounded exotic and had a picture of Swiss mountains. He looked at the box and imagined the freedom of walking among the rocks and the meadows of Switzerland, and so decided to give the *Alpen* a try. *Alpen* turned out to be a muesli of oats, nuts and fruit. And he loved it. Immediately after he'd pushed his empty bowl aside, Louisa came in with a plate of food enough for two. Two slices of fried bread (adding to his fried dinner of the day before), two cooked tomatoes, two fried eggs, two sausages, a small pile of fried mushrooms and some baked beans.

After he wolfed down his breakfast, Ruben decided to would go into town, having no change of clothes or any possessions at all to speak of.

'Where would the town centre be, for shops, clothes and things?' he asked Louisa.

Louisa fetched a small folded map, and pointed to the hotel, moving her finger along the roads as she spoke. 'Turn right out of here, turn down this street here and walk up,' she said. 'You can take this,' she added, and handed the map to Ruben.

'Thank you so much, Louisa. I really appreciate it,'

So relaxed was Ruben after his good night's rest and hearty breakfast, and in the company of Louisa, he'd almost forgotten why he was there in the first place.

'No trouble at all,' replied Louisa sensing something was not quite right with the lad but not wanting to cause trouble or distress. 'Have a safe journey and take care.'

With that, Ruben thanked Louisa and left the hotel, shutting the door behind him. A brief encounter with unlikely strangers who have nothing in common and who might never have met in normal circumstances, and who may never meet again can leave an impression that lasts a lifetime.

Walking along the seafront, Ruben passed decaying nightclubs, closed for the day, and an open front amusement arcade spewing flashing lights and ringing bells onto the street, only a couple of people seemingly playing on the machines inside. The carpet was littered with cigarette stains from long ago. Ruben studied the map and turned down a narrow side street, to be met with a group of pigeons out for a fight. Red brick houses stood crammed in close together with no front gardens, and so quiet it seemed there was no-one at home.

Finally, on the main high street, pedestrianised in an attempt to make the area more pleasant, Ruben saw a row of uninspiring shops. *Oxfam*, *Burtons* and *M&S*, along with a glamorous sounding clothes shop called *Hollywood Fashions*, which in reality sold cheap tat. *Burtons*, being a menswear shop, looked to be the best bet. There wasn't much to choose from. Sometime later, Ruben came out of the shop with some awful jeans, a long-sleeved sweatshirt and some underwear and socks.

It was a job done.

As he continued towards the station, it occurred to Ruben he should really call Dara to tell her he was safe. So what if his phone was tailed? By the time anyone reached Margate he'd be long gone - like any perfect decoy. Dara didn't pick up when he phoned, so he left a message.

Ruben remembered to pre-buy a ticket when he got to the station, and walked up to the ticket office.

'Where to sir?' said the man behind the ticket office window.

'London,' replied Ruben.

'Victoria or St Pancras?'

'I don't know, which is better?'

'It depends on where you want to go,' replied the man, slightly surprised at the question. 'Are you a tourist?'

'Yes,' said Ruben, hesitantly.

'Sure about that?' The man grinned, obviously noting Ruben's American accent.

'Yes,' said Ruben. 'I'm going to a place called Notting Hill'.

'Oh, I see,' continued the man. 'Well, it's much of a muchness. If you go to Victoria you need to take the Victoria line to Oxford Circus and change to the Central line, but you don't want to do that, because it's always so busy. You could go to St Pancras instead and get the Circle line and go straight to Notting Hill but they don't come often and mind you go in the right direction or it really will take forever. Circle Line, see.'

"Whichever is first,' replied Ruben.

'That's Victoria. Single or Return?'

'Single.'

'Are you sure, it's only 50 pence more for a return – any time,' suggested the man.

'Okay' said Ruben bemused. 'I'll take a return. You never know.'

'You never do, sir. You never do.'

Only 50 pence more for the same journey? Britain was a strange country.

Ruben sat on the bench on the platform, leisurely rising to his feet when the train drew into the station. He pressed the button which opened the door after the third attempt. The carriage was almost empty with only a scattering of people sitting separately, seemingly as far from each other as possible, isolated in their own shared space. Ruben was able to stretch out on a six-seat block, and watched the green fields whizz by out of the window, the scene only interrupted by the odd cluster of trees, or small village or town. England was indeed green and compact. No vast spaces with nothing to see but the same open field of corn. Here the scene was ever changing but remaining the same, like the changing of the guard. Ruben took out the address of his distant aunt or dad's cousin, or whatever the relationship was, and planned his route to Notting Hill.

CHAPTER FIFTEEN

At *The Honey Pot,* Dara was trying to understand what had just happened. She knew she hadn't imagined April appearing like she did, but there was still something dreamlike about it. This brief encounter, however, was soon usurped by the absence of Ruben. Even though April explained the reason he had to get away fast, Dara still felt some resentment that he hadn't bothered to say goodbye.

Dara started clearing up the dining area: a missed coffee cup here and there, a dirty table, something unidentifiable on the floor. As she was doing so, a familiar face appeared at the pain of glass in the door.

It was Emilia.

'Hello?' said Dara, almost like a question, hoping Emilia wouldn't vanish as April had.

Emilia knocked on the window: 'The door's locked,' her voice muffled.

Dara forgot she had locked the door and went over to unlock it, starting with the top bolt and working her way down. She was conscious of Emilia scrutinising her whilst she performed this task and felt a bit uneasy despite being pleased to see her.

'Wanna hang?' said Emilia as she entered the cafe.

'I've nothing better to do,' said Dara. 'So, yeah, why not,'

'Great! Come to dinner at mine, I'll show you German suburbia.'

'How far is it?' asked Dara, unsure she had the energy for a long journey, and then having to find home at the end of the night.

'Don't worry, I have a car,' said Emilia, reading Dara's thoughts.

Dara decided she couldn't be bothered with the last few bits of clearing up, so grabbed her bag, turned off the lights and left the cafe. When she turned round from locking the front door, she saw Emilia standing by the open rear door of a large black Mercedes. Although it seemed to Dara like a modern-day Cinderella carriage, she had the feeling it wasn't there to take her to a ball.

'Come on, Dara,' said Emilia. 'In you get.'

As Dara ducked her head to get into the car, she noticed someone else in the back. He was a tall man, thin but with definition and a short white crew cut. He wore some kind of smart khaki uniform with brass buttons. Dara deduced he was someone important in the army, probably the US army, and sat there with the trepidation of someone being summoned to the principal's office.

Emilia climbed in beside her and shut the car door.

The man spoke.

'Hello Dara. My name's Ethan. I'm Emilia's husband. I'm from US Military Intelligence. I've heard a great deal about you.'

'Pleased to meet you,' replied Dara, rather more formally than she intended.

There followed an uncomfortable silence. Dara was lost for words and Ethan was clearly a man of very few.

'So, what are you doing here,' Dara said to Ethan, rather clumsily.

'We were just passing,' said Emilia casually. 'We thought we'd look in.'

'Welcome a fellow American to Berlin,' Ethan continued.

'So do you two always welcome Americans in this way?' said Dara, trying not to sound too confrontational, though that's what she was trying to do. Obviously they didn't lay on the red-carpet treatment for most tourists, so why her?

'Not everyone,' said Emilia, quietly, giving nothing away.

'So you're in Military intelligence then, Ethan? Sounds interesting. What does it involve?' She was trying to dig a little deeper, though was aware it was coming across in something of a rookie manner.

Ethan almost laughed at Dara's awkward attempts at acquiring information, but kept a neutral face.

He explained: 'American's have been stationed in the south of Germany since the end of the Second World War. Also, the south of Berlin. Many settling down and marrying local girls. Germany was divided into four areas after the war, each section occupied by one of the allies: France, the UK, America and Russia. Berlin too was divided into four. After a few years we all relinquished our occupation, apart from Russia.'

'Yes of course. All Americans know that. We are forever being told the Russians are the enemy,' replied Dara.

'Indeed,' continued Ethan. Security was constantly needed in Berlin as it was a part of the Russian territory, and under constant threat. I was stationed in the city when I first signed up around the time the Berlin wall came down. Even after reunification, I just kinda liked it here so we decided to stay, didn't we sweetheart.' Ethan looked at Emilia and held her hand. 'Emilia grew up here.'

'My father was stationed here and met my mom,' said Emilia. I was born here in Germany. I went to school in America but when I came back to visit one year, I met Ethan and we got married.'

'You married young,' remarked Dara, probably inappropriately.

'I suppose,' answered Emilia.

Ethan chimed in, changing the subject to the task in hand and turning his face to look directly at Dara. 'Dara,' he said. 'We need you to go to London. We'll drive you to your apartment. You need to collect your things. No-one will do anything with us there. You will be protected.'

'London?'

'We need you to keep an eye on Justin.'

'You know Justin?'

'We know more about Justin than you might think, Dara,' said Ethan. 'It is very important you do this for us.'

Dara briefly considered April's instructions to stay put, but she was more concerned about Ruben and wanted to go and find him in London, so this seemed like the opportunity to do so.

The chauffeur drove them all to the apartment block, and Dara climbed the stairs to the top. She could hear the horn player playing the now familiar tune. It was louder than usual and seemed more intense. Once in the flat Dara packed a bag and dug out her passport. She was pleasantly surprised to see the gig ticket still there on the table where she'd thrown it, Ruben had left it. Ruben wasn't coming back any time soon, so she grabbed it. At least that was one less thing to worry about, she wouldn't have to blag her way into the gig to spy on Justin. Although blagging her way into gigs was one of her specialities.

The journey down the stairs was a kind of limbo before getting back into the car, escorted by Ethan and Emilia like prison guards, into the unknown. The car, driven by a junior army personnel, drove them out into a residential area of Berlin. Nothing more was revealed about why she was being taken on this journey but Dara had an inkling she was about to find out.

Ethan seemed less intimidating and mysterious than before, and chatted easily to Dara. As the car pulled into the driveway of a large detached house, he made casual conversation.

'This is where we live,' he said. 'It's kind of out of the way. Our own little sanctuary away from it all.'

Dara didn't imagine Ethan had any kind of spiritualism in him to crave a peaceful refuge from the world. As she looked around, she too sensed a place of tranquillity. There were other houses near, but somehow they all seemed so separate and private. As Dara got out of the car, she could hear rustling of leaves and even the rushing of a stream rushing downhill behind the house.

'The house backs onto a small wood, with a stream running through it,' said Emilia. 'It is very beautiful.'

Having spent most of her time living in the city, the sound of rushing streams and the wind rustling through the trees were not sounds Dara had heard much in her life. Any anxieties she had about the bizarre situation she found herself in, dispersed into the woods, leaving her at ease with her new friends, so different to her in every way.

Once inside the house, Dara was shown to a cream coloured sofa on a stark white marbled floor. The rest of the living room was clean and minimal, scrubbed within an inch of its life. Dara sat down carefully so as not to disturb the sofa or push it out of place. Emilia sat on a mirror image sofa opposite. Ethan sat between the two sofas on a black leather swivel armchair. A slight woman entered the room wearing a maid's uniform. To Dara's dread, she was, indeed, a maid.

'Can I get you anything?' she asked formally, but also with the ease of familiarity.

'Some tea, please,' answered Ethan with a similar formal, but friendly voice.

'Thank you,' said Ethan.

The maid dutifully left the room as though in a stage play, as if everything she did was second nature after a number of performances. She returned shortly after carrying a tray with three china cups and a small teapot sitting on it. The maid's outfit added to Dara's sense of watching something rehearsed, that she was part of the drama, somehow, but was yet to be given her lines. Emilia curled her legs up under herself on the sofa in a relaxed, reclined position whilst Dara stayed upright, a contrast to her usual slacker demeanour of lounging apathy.

Ethan turned to Dara.

'I'll get to the point,' he said, seemingly unaware of the maid's presence apart from when she handed him his cup of tea. The maid appeared to Dara the opposite of a ghost, her presence seen but not felt. And Dara still didn't know her name.

The maid remained pouring the tea into the little cups for Dara and Emilia.

Ethan continued: 'Things are not quite going according to plan, Dara. We need to move quickly. You are in great danger if you remain at your apartment. Your cover has been blown.'

'Cover?' said Dara, accidentally saying the word out loud whilst staring hard at Ethan. 'What cover?'

'You may not be aware of why you are here,' explained Ethan in a matter of fact way, without any sense of softening what he was saying. 'We don't know much ourselves, if I'm honest,' he continued. 'What we do know is that you were hired to collect a very important package to take back to America. This package is highly important to us. You would be doing us and your country a great service.'

'I don't understand,' replied Dara.

Ethan continued: 'We are in touch with the man who brought you here. We do not know his identity, but we ask you to help us find him. It is a matter of national importance.'

Dara sipped her tea, looked at the marble floor and said nothing.

'The package involves a US president. You don't want our great country to endure a scandal that could displace America's standing in the world do you?'

'No,' said Dara, 'of course not.' After a while Dara continued. 'Did you organise all this?'

'No,' said Ethan. 'As I said, we are in careful negotiations with our contact - a Russian double agent, long time in our payroll, well MI6's payroll, actually. Us and the Brits are working together on this. Your friend, April, is working here on behalf of her father who is high up in British intelligence. Justin's father is too, but in a minor role. We thought bringing April and Justin in to help would prove useful as they would blend in. Just another British couple in Berlin. So we set them up in the cafe, but they didn't seem to be getting anywhere. Our contact has the package but isn't giving it to us. We don't know if he has gone rogue, or what he is doing. Our relationship with him goes back decades but he disappeared years ago. We thought he was dead and that the Russians had taken the package back. But then he emerged not long ago. He'd been watching us all along. He wasn't convinced we wouldn't double cross him, so he said he would organise something and we were to await instructions. We don't usually work this way but he has us over a barrel. We needed to show him we are on his side, so we did what he said. We organised an apartment for you as directed by our contact and planted the brochures that led you to *The Honey Pot*. He must have a contact State side to have organised things that end, but we don't know who. We don't know the nature of his relationship with the Brits yet. We work together but we are not necessarily on the same side.'

'I see,' said Dara, 'this really was a set up. So we've been duped?'

'Don't say that,' said Emilia, finally speaking up after listening intently to her husband. 'You're doing great. You have no idea how well you are doing.'

'But how was our cover blown?' cried Dara suddenly. 'Who was it?'

'Ah,' said Ethan, 'that we don't know.'

'Where's Ruben?' said Dara, becoming agitated.

'We believe Ruben is okay. He is hiding out at a British seaside town. He'll head to London, we are sure. We know he has family there.

'Do you think April could have blown our cover?'

'She ran, even from us. We have no sign of her. We do not suspect it was April who blew your cover. We expect she's laying low, for her own reasons.'

Dara pulled herself together and started to converse with Ethan on his level.

'So, tell me again what you need me to do.'

'You have to get to London,' said Ethan, looking at Dara without dropping his gaze.

'And what is it you need me to do there, exactly?'

'We want you to catch up with Ruben in London, if you can. But it's more likely he will find you first. In the meantime we need you to find Justin. Our suspicion is he's up to something and he's likely to be in touch with Ruben at some point. We need you to act like you're there to do some sight-seeing whilst you wait for Ruben, but really we want you to look out for any behaviours in Justin that are odd. Anything. Make a note of it even if you think it is unimportant. Tell us who he meets, what he says, where he goes. Anything you can.'

Dara took a sip of tea.

'Justin's always odd,' she said. 'If there's anything that doesn't add up, I'll let you know.'

'Thank you, Dara,' said Ethan.

'I know where he'll be tomorrow. It'll be the perfect way to watch him unawares. He may let his guard down.'

'How do you know where he'll be?' said Emilia.

'He'd organised for him and Ruben to see *The Cardiacs* at the *Astoria*.'

Emilia and Ethan looked at each other, a puzzled look on their faces.

'They're a band. The *Astoria* is where they're playing. It's in London.'

Dara got Ruben's ticket for the show out of her bag and held it up for Ethan and Emilia to see.

'Ah,' Emilia and Ethan both said at once.

'Won't he see you?' said Emilia.

'Na,' replied Dara. 'I'll think of something.'

'Great, you're really getting into this,' said Ethan, impressed.

Ethan told Dara he'd organised accommodation in London and handed her a piece of paper with the address.

'I've asked April's dad to work on me with this,' he said.

'April's dad?'

'MI6, remember,' said Ethan. 'Keep up.' He then reached down beside his armchair and handed Dara a travel pack containing an open-ended plane ticket, an A-Z map of London and some cash in pounds sterling. 'Keep these safe,' he said.

Dara spent an uneventful evening watching films with Emilia and Ethan, looking only slightly less intimidating in his casual wear.

Later that night, Dara lay awake in bed, planning. She couldn't go to the gig as she was in case Justin saw her. She would need a disguise. How to get a disguise? But it had been a long day, and she felt her eyes closing over. She'd worry about the disguise when she got to London.

Dara was rushed through the check-out and security at Berlin Brandenburg airport, and straight to the first-class lounge. It seemed there were some perks working for military intelligence. She imagined a buffet of fine foods waiting for her, and maybe some wine. When she got there, she remembered her previous experience on her way to Berlin with Ruben, right at the beginning of this adventure. You could, however, drink any kind of alcohol - wine, champagne, gin, whisky - anything at all. And people did. At ten in the morning! Dara was no longer shocked but decided not to participate. She thought herself on the rebellious side, but even she wouldn't drink alcohol in the morning, or at any time unless it was on her night off and she was in a bar socialising or at a gig.

A middle-aged man poured himself a red wine and asked Dara if she would like something. Dara politely declined. She sat down. Was she being too conservative? Maybe she wasn't as rebellious as she'd always thought.

The middle-aged man sidled up to her and sat next to her.

'Where are you off to?' he asked in a soft, slightly creepy, voice. It was obviously a line, like 'Do you come here often?' only in an airport lounge rather than a nightclub. Like all men in this situation, the man wasn't really interested in the answer, he just wanted an excuse to get closer to her. 'On business?' he continued, when Dara didn't reply immediately.

'Sort of,' replied Dara, instantly regretting it.

'What sort of business?' the man answered. He was getting closer, his leg touching hers, his hand touching her arm. Dara knew she had to stop this short. He was irritating her and she just wanted to be alone.

'Nothing,' she said curtly, and moved seats.

The man didn't bother her again. He took a newspaper from a table - *The Financial Times*, a curious pink colour - sat down, opened it and hid behind its curious pink pages, large enough, it seemed to Dara, to cover his entire body.

The flight passed without much incident apart from the same man from the lounge sitting on the row next to Dara. He must have been in his late 60s, and started chatting to her, or rather chatting her up, before the plane had even taken off.

'Are you travelling for business or pleasure,' said the man once again in a soft voice.

'Business,' came Dara's short reply.

'What is it that you do, young lady? You look very glamorous. It must be something interesting.'

'I'm wearing black jeans and sneakers and a plain shirt, but if you think that's glamorous, well okay,' replied Dara, slightly sarcastically.

'And what is it that you do for work?' the man continued.

'I work in a café in Berlin,' came Dara's reply, deciding against going into details but this made the man continue his moves. He put his hand on her knee, forcing Dara onto the front foot.

'Okay mister, you got me. I work for the FBI.'

The man assumed she was joking and took umbrage at this brush off and removed his hand quickly. He didn't say another word to her the rest of the flight, even when she asked him if he could let her by when she wanted to go to the bathroom. He simply pulled his legs inwards without a word and let her pass by. He even ignored the lady on the other side of him, a similar age to himself. It made for an awkward atmosphere, and Dara was relieved when the plane landed in London.

There was no smart black limo waiting for Dara at the other end, so she had to make her own way to her destination. Taking out the piece of paper with the address of April's father, she looked up the address on the A-Z map. She saw a subway stop called Archway, which seemed to be closest to the address. Looking around for transport, she saw a sign to the Underground station. Surprised, but relieved, that the Underground came all the way out to the airport, she headed down the escalator and looked at the Underground map on the wall just inside the entrance. As she was doing so, a man who worked for the Underground, seeing she was staring at the map, approached her.

'Can I help you madam?' he asked.

'I'm trying to get to Archway,' said Dara, humouring him. She could do this on her own, but it made a change for a man to be talking to her without creeping her out.

'You need to take the Piccadilly line in dark blue and change to the Northern Line in black at either Leicester Square or King's Cross,' the man explained.

'Which is better?' asked Dara.

'It depends,' replied the man. 'Leicester Square is always busy - tourists, you know. But King's Cross is full of commuters, so that's busy as well. King's Cross is a mainline train station, but you've just missed the evening rush hour, so it'll probably be not too bad.'

'Thanks,' said Dara. 'I'll go for Kings Cross.'

Dara got on the train that pulled into the station. She watched the people get on and off as the train made its way to King's Cross. Each leg of the journey saw a different set of people. At first it was people with large suitcases arriving from their homelands. Then some local people in scruffy clothes got on and off three stops later. Then an influx of groups of students and teenagers with backpacks, speaking in languages Dara couldn't understand. This all was new to her, and she began to feel like a fish out of water. King's Cross took almost an hour to get to. And by the time she reached Archway, she was almost completely disoriented. She stepped out onto the street - grateful for the fresh air - and looked at the A-Z. The address still seemed far, but she was determined to make her way on foot - to wake her up as much as anything else. After walking the wrong way and then uphill, having to come back down the hill and walk in the opposite direction, Dara eventually reached April's dad's house as the sun began to set.

She didn't even have to knock on the door before the light in the hallway came on. A man in his 60s opened the door and said in a friendly, welcoming voice: 'You must be Dara, come on in.'

It had been so long since Dara had heard any kind words that she was quite taken aback, and looked in wonderment as she entered the warmly lit house with comfortable seating and an inviting kitchen.

'You must be hungry,' said the man. 'Help yourself to anything in the fridge. By the way, I'm Geoffrey, April's dad, I expect she's told you all about me.'

Dara nodded: 'A little.'

Dara sat on a kitchen chair and felt vulnerable at being in a stranger's house, yet somehow safe, like a child - quite unlike her usual confidently cool character. She ate a bowl of soup with a crusty buttered roll that Geoffrey had heated up for her, and cup of tea, quite unlike anything she'd drunk in the US or Germany. Quickly, Dara felt warm and cosy in this place. Geoffrey showed her to a bedroom upstairs before asking in a casual way: 'I don't suppose you know where April is, do you?'

'I'm afraid not,' replied Dara, with caution. It was not the news he would want to hear or she would want to tell.

'Ah, thank you,' replied Geoffrey, as casually as he'd asked the question, though Dara guessed he was not so calm under the surface.

Dara scanned her bedroom. A large Victorian bed with white linen took up most of the space and on one wall there was an unused fireplace. The sash window looked over the garden. Dara didn't have the energy to ponder over April's whereabouts, what part her father might play in all this, or even how she managed to get herself here. Within moments of her head hitting the pillow, she was fast asleep.

CHAPTER SIXTEEN

When Dara awoke the next day, the house was empty, yet it seemed so full of life. The windows rattled as the wind swirled around outside, leaves picked up by the wind were thrown on the window panes making a rustling sound as though someone was walking on them, trying not to be heard. The light of the bright sun shone through, exposing the dust which danced in the air so vividly that you could imagine the sounds inaudible to the human ear. There was a whirlwind and then a dull thud from the kitchen as the washing machine spun the clothes dry, then ground to a halt. There was a constant hum of a fridge, old and cranky.

Dara found a note stuck to the fridge door.

'We've gone out for a family day. A picnic on Hampstead Heath. We thought we'd leave you asleep but do come and find us if it's not too late for your next mission. We're on Parliament Hill. Do help yourself to anything.'

Next mission? thought Dara. *Who did they think she was?* The note was in stark contrast to the formal ceremony at Ethan and Emilia's. Despite no maid permanently placed to serve, the empty house still seemed alive and friendly. This was a place where you had to do things for yourself, make your own decisions, be independent. Perhaps it was because this way of living was how she lived, she felt more at ease here.

Whilst making coffee and toast, Dara wondered what to do next. The first thing she needed to do was let Ruben know where she was. Not wanting to use her cell phone, in case someone was listening in, she used the house phone, and rang Ruben's number. The call went straight to voicemail.

'Ruben,' she said, 'it's me. I'm in London.'

Dara didn't want to take the chance of saying any more, and placed the receiver back in its cradle. At least he would know he wasn't alone.

The invitation to Parliament Fields seemed like fun but aside from the fact she had no idea where that was, time was passing rapidly. The gig was tonight and she needed to put her plan into action.

Dara jumped on the Underground and aimed for Oxford Street - the world famous shopping street - taking a train on the Piccadilly line, the dark blue line on the Underground map. The journey seemed to go on forever. Eventually she reached her destination.

Black taxis and red London buses filled the road, moving slowly. A bus would stop at a bus stop and the taxi behind would attempt to go around it but invariably had to wait impatiently until the bus moved again. There were so many people too, many of them on the sidewalk and crossing the road any place they could - not just at the crossings. They walked in front of buses, cars and sometimes taxis - none of whom bothered to stop, causing pedestrians to leap out of the way, shopping bags flying. Everyone seemed in a rush. Not the gentile England she had seen in films. Shops were a mixture of generic clothes stores, familiar chain stores, department stores that looked so dull on the outside, she wondered what could possibly be inside.

Crammed between these huge stores were tacky boutiques selling cheap punk/goth clothes, the grating outside displaying accessories, including several that sold brightly coloured wigs. Dara stopped at one of these tacky shops and picked out a bright red wig, a bob with a straight fringe. *This will have to do*, she thought, *at least it wasn't green or pink*. Her plan was to wear a wig such as this to draw attention from her face. Hiding in plain sight. From what she knew of *The Cardiacs*, she wouldn't be the only one at the gig with hair like this.

Dara needed to put on some heavy make-up to complete the look. One of the department stores must have a bathroom. So she went into the nearest one: *Debenhams*. As she entered the huge store, she could almost smell the depression. It wasn't oppressive, just dull and lifeless. There didn't seem to be many people in the vast shop. At the front of the shop were the make-up counters. All the usual grown-up brands - *Chanel, Elizabeth Arden, Clarines* - all managing to look decidedly unglamorous considering their high-end chic reputation. Perhaps it was just the shop. You could stick Lady Gaga in here and she'd look drab.

Dara hovered around the make-up counters, without much hope and suddenly saw a flash of bright red hair - almost like the wig she'd just bought, but from a bottle, not something picked up in a tacky shop - coming towards her. In the way the young woman sauntered over, she recognised a kindred spirit. A goth girl beneath the uniform. The two made eye contact. Brush in hand, the cool girl came up to Dara and offered to do her make-up.

'I was going to do my own,' said Dara, 'To be honest, I wasn't planning on buying anything. I'm going to a gig later.'

'Hey no worries', said the shop assistant, the badge on the front of the uniform telling Dara her name was Claire. 'Sit up here. I'll see you right.'

Dara sat on the high stool while Claire scuttled around her, stroking her face with various different brushes. It was quite relaxing being pampered for a time. It all felt so normal. Dara wanted to say 'what's a nice girl doing in a dull place like this,' and found herself doing so.

'I used to work in *Harrods*, but it's less serious here. They can't see you've been up all night,' said Claire with a cheeky grin. 'There you go, all done.'

With time on her hands, Dara asked Claire where the best shopping was on Oxford Street.

'You wanna go to *Selfridges*,' said Claire. 'It's a few blocks up. Cross over Regents street, and you can't miss it.'

'Thanks,' replied Dara, hoping she would bump into Claire again. Not wanting to get too close to strangers, however, she said goodbye and went on her way.

'Enjoy the gig,' Claire called after her.

Dara carried on up Oxford Street, and crossed where Regent Street fed into it. She saw the designer shops of *Ralph Lauren* and *Yves Saint Laurent*, and out of the corner of her eye down a side street, she could just make out *Vivienne Westwood*. That was cool. Towering over her, however, stood *Selfridges*, its colourful and dynamic display in the huge windows telling her there was something exciting inside. Dara looked through the huge sets of revolving doors and saw the same make-up counters and the same clothes concessions as *Debenhams*, but presented with poise and glamour. She also saw an enchanted wood of clothes racks with accessories for leaves. Not as good as *Macy's* but not far off.

Next to *Selfridges*, Dara noticed a small alleyway, the sign informing her it was called St Christopher's Place. Only in England would there be such a small street next to such a grand building. Dara walked down the alley, looking in the windows of the little shops there, an interesting contrast to the vast spaces of Oxford Street. At the end of the alley, Dara came to a courtyard with a few restaurants, and realised she had hardly eaten a thing all day. She sat down on the terrace of a lovely looking Italian place, called *Carluccios* and ordered a pasta dish and a glass of white wine (everyone seemed to be drinking a glass), and felt ever so sophisticated.

This was a place to chill out - something she really needed at the moment - and so she did until it was time to get to the gig.

When it was time to go, Dara got the *A-Z* from her bag as she sipped on another glass of wine, and discovered the *Astoria* was only five minutes down the road. She could have walked, but her new found air of elegance and composure, and the realisation she had some free cash, plus the wine flowing through her, encouraged Dara to hail a black taxi. She would arrive in style.

Dara got out of the cab at Tottenham Court Road Station, and there in front of her stood the *Astoria*. This was where Justin was supposed to be. It looked like her kind of place, a grungy gig venue, but not the sort of place someone like Justin would even know existed. The awning gave the name of the band playing. *The Cardiacs*. An old boyfriend was a fan of this British Band, and many others. Really freaky music, even for her but great also. Again, Justin at this gig just didn't seem to add up. But then she suspected he wasn't there for the music. She felt like she was in some kind of spy in a film in her synthetic wig. Then she thought about April's disappearance, Ruben on the run, being involved with US Military Intelligence and MI6? And whatever Justin was. Suddenly, it wasn't fun anymore. What on earth had her and Ruben walked into?

The disguise was obviously ridiculous and almost comical but under the circumstances it would have to do. Having had a previous interest with the London punk scene, and having some knowledge of the venue and the band, Dara had the vague idea she may just blend in by sticking out. The 'Hiding in plain sight' thing. It was a pity she wasn't there to see the gig, thought Dara, but she consoled herself by saying that there would be another time.

Armed with Ruben's ticket, Dara went up to the ticket office. Groups of three, four and five, and more, hung around the door and just inside. Going to a gig alone was always a conspicuous thing to do. But Dara couldn't help that. Still, her paranoia set in, and Dara was convinced people were staring at her and wondering who she was and why she was alone. A few guys looked at her for other reasons, too shy to approach, and a couple of ladies made complementary remarks about Dara hair to each other, just out of her earshot, so all Dara could sense were some mumbles and stares.

The room was beginning to fill up with people, all of whom were mainly ignoring the echoey, barely recognisable music being played by the DJ. Then she spotted him. Justin. He wasn't in disguise, so he stuck out somewhat. If only he had thought to change his appearance, he may not have been seen by Dara, but this was no place for posh hipsters. Justin appeared to be standing next to

113

someone and conversing sporadically. He then seemed to give some sort of package to his acquaintance.

Dara then noticed another couple of men, also remarkable by being unremarkable. She had seen them before. One was definitely the person Ruben had described as tailing him and who had spooked April. Did these people only have one set of clothes? They too were looking around and appeared to finally spot Justin, and started towards him. Something caught the light and Dara saw one of them was holding a knife.

At that very moment, however, the band started up. The music was like a fairground ride in a horror film. Jerky and loud, twisting and turning. All of a sudden the crowd burst forth and started jumping up and down to the music, pushing and shoving - in other words, moshing. A familiar sight to Dara, but to the two men after Justin, it was unfamiliar and completely unexpected. Perplexed at the sight of so many people, including girls, seemingly fighting but not, the man with the knife snarled and pushed through the crowd. But when the song ended, he returned to where he'd started from, empty handed and still angry.

Justin, and the man he was speaking to were nowhere to be seen.

Dara didn't want to stare at the pursuers in case they stared back and realised who she was, but out of the corner of her eye, she noticed them having a heated discussion. As she was looking, she seemed to be the only one in the place who noticed the knife flicker again. One man seemed to begin slipping to the ground, but the other caught him and dragged him outside, muttering something to the unaware front of house staff as he left, probably saying his friend was drunk, or something. It was something they would have seen a million times before, so would have suspected nothing.

Dara didn't dare follow. Justin was probably long gone and whilst she didn't catch of *what* he had handed over, but she *had* seen him there and definitely saw some kind of hand over going on. This was the important factor. It was proof that he had followed through on his plan to deceive April. Dara felt a pang of hatred towards Justin for duping not only her and Ruben, but also his wife, Dara's friend. There was nothing she could do now but to stay put in case anyone was waiting around outside. So she stayed and tried to enjoy the rest of the gig as best she could.

Warned not to use her phone, Dara remembered April had told her that in the UK there were things called mini cabs. They had offices in various places and instead of hailing one, like you would a yellow taxi in the US or a black cab in London, you went up to the kiosk and asked for a minicab to your destination. No phones involved and cash only, price agreed beforehand so no surprises or scenic routes. Normally, Dara would have sussed out where one of these places might be, but she had not had time. She stepped out onto the street with trepidation, hoping the whereabouts of a minicab office would be obvious. She was soon relieved to see two such places, one right next to the venue. Having left as soon as the gig finished, she had no trouble booking a ride.

'That's £12.50 love', said the receptionist. 'Ivan will be with you shortly'.

Dara found it odd that she was quoted a price beforehand but when the car swung round to greet her and she climbed in, she soon found out the cab had no metre. This was just too easy, and Dara wondered what the catch was. But there was no catch, and she found herself headed to April's family home for the night, shaken but relieved things hadn't gone worse than they had.

The next morning Dara awoke with the sun streaming onto her face and the sound of the clutter of crockery. She ventured out of her bedroom, stepped lightly down the stairs and entered the kitchen.

'Ah you're awake,' said Geoffrey, seemingly excited to see her. 'We thought we'd let you sleep in. You've had a trying time of late, haven't you?'

Trying, thought Dara, that's an understatement. She was also slightly confused about how she got home. She traced her steps. She was at the gig, she remembered getting into the minicab. She was so tired and exhausted, she had no idea how she managed to direct the driver to the right address.

Geoffrey turned to a little woman with long grey hair standing by the sink who gave a big smile and said in a calm and gentle voice, 'It's been a tough time, hasn't it, dear?'

Dara wasn't sure who this lady was, or how she knew anything about her, but she nodded obediently.

'I'm Maggie,' the grey-haired lady said, then precisely making sure Dara understood exactly who she was, added, 'Geoffrey's wife, April's mum. There's still some toast on the table with various jams and butter. Do help yourself.'

So Dara helped herself, and started eating. At that point a youth barely out of his teens burst into the kitchen, barely acknowledging Dara, as though it was completely normal to have a stranger at the breakfast table. He picked up a couple of pieces of toast, put them on a plate he grabbed out of the cupboard and marched back out of the room, as though hoping to have come and gone incognito.

'That was our youngest, Paul,' said Geoffrey. 'You may get a grunt out of him one of these days.' He gave Maggie a wink and both laughed.

On another occasion Dara might have been nauseated by the friendly and amiable nature that only the comfortably off have, had she not been so utterly grateful for their hospitality and their provision of a safe haven.

Maggie left the kitchen and returned with a towel, a dressing gown, a pair of slippers and a bar of soap.

'You'll feel better after a nice hot bath, dear, she said, handing Dara everything she had.

'Take your time,' said Geoffrey. 'I expect you have a great deal to tell me.' He pointed to another room which appeared to be the living room. 'I'll be in there when you're ready.'

Upstairs, Dara shut the bathroom door and climbed into the ready drawn hot bath and relaxed, taking the time to herself while she could.

CHAPTER SEVENTEEN

Geoffrey led Dara into the living room where she sat down on a slightly decaying green sofa. It was comfortable, with thick cushions that sank into the rest of the sofa when Dara sat on them. Geoffrey pretended not to notice and took a seat in the armchair opposite.

Maggie came in carrying a tray with mugs of tea and small plates with walnut biscuits on.

'I thought you'd like something to keep you going,' she remarked, before putting the tray down on the coffee table in front of the sofa, handing Dara a mug of tea and a small plate of biscuits. Dara didn't know what to take first, so took them both.

'Thank you so much,' replied Dara in an attempt at a British accent, doing her best to be polite in the company of such grand people.

The mug of tea was hotter than expected and Dara spilled a bit on the sofa. Maggie pretended not to notice.

'I'll leave you to it,' Maggie said.

'That's grand, my love,' said Geoffrey tenderly to her.

Dara was fascinated by the way Geoffrey and Maggie spoke to each other so calmly. So different from her own family - so full of anxiety and bickering. It made her sad at the life she might have missed.

'I'll be in the library doing some work if you need me,' said Maggie, as she floated out of the room.

'You have a library?' said Dara.

'It's not a real one,' joked Maggie with a short laugh, just about audible from the corridor. 'It's just where we put most of our books.'

Geoffrey turned to Dara, a serious look on his face.

'I suppose you want to know what this is all about, don't you? Who I am? April? Justin? What has April told you so far?'

'Told me?' Dara was slightly aghast. Her ordeal at the gig had been so dramatic she couldn't even begin to comprehend its magnitude let alone recount the incident to Geoffrey as though she was describing her day at work.

'I, I -' Dara stumbled.

'What is it you know about April?' he said, gently

'When we got to Berlin, I mean Ruben and I - Ruben is my boyfriend - we somehow ended up in their cafe. Justin and April's cafe. April and Justin were the first people we met. We were quite lost in many ways. They were so friendly. They made us feel welcome and gave us a reason to be there other than our mission.

'Which was?'

Dara started to recount the story: 'On vacation we found an envelope at a gas station. I suppose I could have just chucked it but it seemed almost to have been written for me. I can't explain. Life was so tedious with work - I'd been working at Starbucks after college. I then got a job in a clothes shop but I just didn't know what I wanted to do. All I knew was I needed a change. Well I certainly got that. Be careful what you wish for, as they say. But you know this right?'

'Not all, I want to hear it from you. Do go on,' said Geoffrey.

'There were plane tickets to Berlin in the envelope which I found, believe it or not, at a remote gas station! There's no way we would ever have been be able to afford to go to Europe, not now, not ever. This was such an opportunity.' She lowered her voice, as if what she had to say next was difficult for her to relay. 'All we had to do was find a package and bring it back. The owner couldn't go himself,'

'Was that it?' enquired Geoffrey.

'There was a reward,' Dara continued.

'Weren't you worried?' asked Geoffrey

'No, it happens,' Dara tried to justify. 'I mean if it was drugs, we'd know. It was just some papers, or something. Ruben was sceptical but he became so enthused by the idea of a trip to Berlin. It just made a lot of sense. This guy said in a note in the envelope that he was too ill to travel and the package needed to be collected from a safety deposit box, so they couldn't use a courier service. Besides, apparently the content was too confidential. It happens all the time in the States. My friend took some valuables across the state line when she was travelling, it was cheaper than using a commercial company, and safer. No-one knew, no-one suspected a college student driving a beaten up mustang. So we thought no-one would suspect a young couple on vacation, or travelling round Europe. Besides, we could always pull out. What was the worst that could happen?'

Of course, Geoffrey knew exactly what was going on. He'd had a hand in setting the whole thing up. Not all was quite going to plan. There was something amiss, but he couldn't put his finger quite on what.

'April gave us a job so we could hang out in Berlin more. Ruben wanted to explore his roots as his grandmother is from there. We wanted to stay. We *needed* to stay as we couldn't work out where this deposit box was and we didn't know the code. We just assumed the instructions on how to find it would just be there waiting for us. We thought we were just missing something. Justin and April were great fun and we hung out loads,' Dara continued. Particularly at *The White Russian*. We had -'

'Tell me about that,' said Geoffrey. 'In as much detail as you can.'

'We were regulars. The owners knew April and Justin, and got to know us too. The clubs are amazing in Berlin too.' Dara stopped, checking herself. Best not to go there with April's father.

'*The White Russian . . .*' Geoffrey said, getting Dara back on track.

'Yes, of course. I'm sorry. There were some interesting characters, for sure. So different from America, but you can see the same traits...' she digressed, and noticing Geoffrey's forehead form a little frown of frustration, she bought herself back to topic. 'We were noticing some peculiar incidents, but we shrugged them off. We thought it was just

Berlin, you know. But Ruben saw April really spooked one day after seeing someone in the cafe. It was someone Ruben recognised too. He'd seen him hanging about. We thought he was following Ruben. When April recognised him and got spooked, I got really scared. Then I saw Justin speaking to him when I was coming back from work, like they knew each other.'

'You mean the man who spooked April and who you thought was following Ruben, was known to Justin?

'It's why I came to London,'

'Back up, Dara,' said Geoffrey, the information that Justin knew this mystery man seeming to have agitated him.

'Sorry,' said Dara. 'I'm jumping forwards a bit. I just can't explain but I knew something was wrong. Justin had told April when April got spooked in the bar that he didn't know the guy, yet here he was speaking to him. April and Justin seemed so solid, as a couple, I mean. Why would he lie? 'Then all that crap happened with April, and Justin was supposed to be going to London with Ruben, but Ruben had to take off. So I just grabbed the concert ticket that was meant for him. I was a day or so behind Justin but I knew where he would be.'

Dara thought it best at the moment not to let Geoffrey know about her involvement with Ethan, as she wasn't sure she was meant to make that known.

'Was he there?' asked Geoffrey innocently, seemingly a little less agitated. 'Justin?'

'Yes'

'Doing what?'

'I don't know, talking to someone, I saw them exchange a package.'

'A package?' said Geoffrey, suddenly leaning forwards and putting his cup down directly on the table making a thud unexpectedly loud for a small cup. Some tea splashed over the rim and onto the table creating a small pool of brown liquid. Geoffrey didn't seem to notice or if he did, made no attempt to clean it up so the liquid just sat there, uninvited and out of place, a blot on the landscape. 'Who was he? The man Justin gave the package to. Can you describe him?'

'I mean he looked like the other guys at the gig, Justin did not. Oh, and the guy who had spooked April and followed Ruben in Berlin, he was there too, in London, with someone else. Another Russian, I think. I think they were both Russian. One of them had a knife, they were clearly going for Justin and the other man, but they couldn't get to them. I think one of them then stabbed the other. Not sure who stabbed who. I didn't want to look, in case they recognised me, even in my wig. I've been to some rough gigs in my time but this......'

Something was slowly dawning on Geoffrey.

'Maggie, come here.'

Maggie came running in, she had a facade of calm but underneath it was clear she was getting a bit nervous. Dara meanwhile didn't know what Maggie had to do with things but at least she'd had her gut feeling about Justin confirmed. Geoffrey seemed to be onto something too.'

'Thomas Pringle, Maggie. A pal of yours, was he not?'

Maggie replied, her face colouring a little. 'Yes, sort of. He was my friend's brother,'

'And the rest, my dear,' said Geoffrey, his previous calm demeanour towards his wife disappearing by the second, 'and romantic liaison, I seem to remember.'

'Yes okay,' said Maggie, 'but that's in the past long before we got together. We've been through this before, my darling. What of it?'

'It suddenly dawned on me - his father, Rupert. He must be the Sixth Man.'

Curiously, Maggie didn't argue. Dara had no clue what they were talking about and wanted to ask what was this 'Sixth Man' thing, but felt it wasn't for her to ask. She realised how different her persona had become at this moment - timid and shy - not like her at all, and she didn't like it. It wasn't like her to shy away from a confrontation.

'I don't understand,' she blurted out. 'Please can you tell me what you are talking about?'

Geoffrey was only slightly taken aback at Dara's outburst, and continued.

'Rupert is Justin's grandfather. My older brother, Cam, was at Cambridge with Rupert's son Thomas - Justin's uncle.' Looking at the expression on Dara's face, Geoffrey added with a smile, 'I know. It's a little complicated.'

Dara raised her eyebrows. 'You're telling me,' she said.

'I remember Thomas well,' Geoffrey said. 'I was a bit in awe of him, to be honest. Or scared. I've never been sure. I was in the year below my brother and Thomas at Cambridge. He was a big lad. I was only a wee fella and what with me being Cam's little brother, Thomas looked out for me. Maggie had an infatuation with him too. Didn't you, dear?'

Maggie blushed a little.

'I could tell, you know,' Geoffrey said. 'Even then.'

'Geoffrey,' said Maggie, 'please.'

Geoffrey smiled at his wife a little, although to Dara, it didn't seem to be the warmest of smiles.

Geoffrey continued.

'MI5 and MI6 recruited from Oxford and Cambridge, Thomas and Cam among them. Some of the new recruits formed a spy ring and became double agents. Three members of the spy ring were discovered whilst Cam was there in the 60s. It turned out the Russians had been infiltrating the place for years. Cam had a feeling not all the double agents there had been picked up. He was convinced there was someone else. He was right. Actually, two more were discovered over the next few years, bringing the total to five. Cam still thought there was one more - someone close to him - the Sixth Man. He was sure of it. Thomas said Cam was imagining things, but I knew he was lying. Maggie, you must have known something?'

'Thomas, silly Tommy. I thought he'd grown out of it. It was the 60s and we were so full of ideals. Thomas seemed so glamorous with his secret meetings and ideas about changing the world. I think he got a bit fed up with first year like me on his tail, but it was just the times.'

'I bet he did,' said Geoffrey, sarcastically.

'Geoffrey,' said Maggie, her face flush of earlier embarrassment replaced with a flush of anger. 'that's enough.

Geoffrey locked eyes with her for a split second, then looked down at his hands.

'Sorry, dear,' he said. 'Please continue.'

'Thank you,' Maggie replied. 'Times changed. Ideals changed. We all grew up,'

Dara still didn't know how any of this was relevant: 'So you think Thomas was the other double agent, and Justin has carried on the 'family profession'?'

Geoffrey nodded, solemnly.

'Someone knew the identity of our double agent in Berlin. It must be the Sixth Man - or someone he is handling. It is how the Kremlin lost the incriminating telegram. How much do you know about this?' added Geoffrey, quite sharply.

Dara shrank in her seat, wondering how much she should reveal. 'I know about a valuable paper with important information.'

'This is really serious Dara,' replied Geoffrey gravely. 'You must tell me everything.'

'You mean the telegram?'

'Not just a telegram, Dara. It is a telegram that could implicate a US President in a very unfavourable light.'

Dara thought it best to feign ignorance at this point.

'I didn't know that!' exclaimed Dara. 'What are you talking about? Which President? All I knew was that it was a telegram.'

Geoffrey thought about telling Dara more, but thought better of it as at this stage. If it was all new to her, he didn't know how she would react and it could put her in jeopardy. So he avoided the question by continuing.

'The Yanks have wiped it from their records, it would just be too much of a scandal, I hope you understand.'

'I suppose,' said Dara, a little disappointed Geoffrey didn't tell her. 'I understand.'

At this point Maggie interjected, more a distraction trying to prevent either Geoffrey revealing the scandal in full to Dara or Dara retreating in disappointment.

'We helped in retrieving the evidence from Russia, via our Russian agent but he never passed it over. Even I don't know who he is, but I know everyone's after him.'

Like a relay, Maggie passed the conversation back to Geoffrey.

'The Russians want the telegram back, so they can use it to bend the Americans over a barrel, should they need to. They will certainly kill our contact for being a double agent. They'll never forgive him for that. The cold war may have ceased but old scores never die, even now.

'Poor guy,' said Dara, exposing her naivety, the empathic nature of someone unused to the spying game.

Geoffrey and Maggie paused for a moment, touched by Dara's innocent comment, almost ashamed of their own aloof attitude.

'Indeed,' muttered Geoffrey, speaking for both himself and Maggie. 'It's important to remember we are dealing with human beings, we are not animals to be hunted, any of us.'

'Hunting animals isn't right either,' said Dara. 'Animals have feelings too - and families.'

Maggie nodded, sympathetically.

'But animals hunt when they need to,' replied Geoffrey. 'And so do people.'

Dara felt like a child suddenly being told about the horrors of adult life. Perhaps retreating into a more innocent version of herself, the more she was exposed to this potentially dangerous lifestyle.

Maggie continued the story: 'MI6 are helping the Americans get hold of the telegram so it doesn't get exposed.

Geoffrey took over. 'We have the agent contact and besides, it makes us look good,'

'Win some brownie points,' replied Maggie. 'Talking of which, I'm getting hungry. Anyone want some walnut cake?'

'That would be lovely,' replied Geoffrey.

Not knowing whether she wanted walnut cake or not, Dara replied: 'Yes, please.' It was perplexing that there was only this one flavour on offer but at least there was continuity in the flavour of their confections.

Whilst Maggie was out of the room, Geoffrey said. 'We know the agent has defected but he lives in the shadows. His identity and whereabouts have always escaped us. A pity, he thinks we want to kill him, but really we want to protect him.'

'I guess Justin is now the double agent, carrying on from Thomas?' asked Dara wanting to contribute.

'I'm beginning to think so. Being married to April he would have known our plan. Our plan with you and Ruben to help find the agent and the telegram.'

Dara interjected again: 'Justin was planning to stitch up Ruben, I'm sure, or use him here as cover. And why would he have secret liaisons behind April's back?'

'He's up to something, that's for sure,' said Geoffrey.

At that point, Maggie walked through the door carrying a tray with little plates of cake and tiny forks.

'Such a naive one,' she said. 'I don't suppose he knows what his actions will do.'

Geoffrey continued: 'Thomas is behind it for sure. It has his name all over it. Justin wouldn't do this without his father's support.'

'I found it odd Justin would use a punk rock gig as cover. I didn't think he'd be into that sort of thing,' mused Dara.

'Thomas always hung with the rebellious crowd,' replied Geoffrey. 'Even into middle age. Probably some of that rubbed off on his son. I'll bet Justin stuck out like a sore thumb, though. Just like Thomas used to.'

As Maggie handed out the plates of cake she remarked: 'Justin's a terrible liar. To let you suspect him, what a rookie mistake. I'm surprised Thomas put him in such danger. But then again, I'm not.'

At that point, Paul walked in: 'Dara, your phone is ringing upstairs.'

Dara rushed to her room, her phone flashing up a missed call from Ruben.

CHAPTER EIGHTEEN

Ruben thought about his next move. The last call he'd made to Dara had used up the tiny amount of battery he had left. His phone was dead. So, first thing would be to get a charger and charge the thing up. He managed to find a phone shop in the town centre. Ruben then made his way back to the hotel and asked Louisa if he could quickly use a plug socket. Louise was happy to oblige, and Ruben waited till all the bars on his phone were full. It might be some time till he could get to charge it again, so he didn't take any chances. When the phone was ready, Ruben switched it on. A beep and a message that a voicemail had been left. Ruben accessed the voicemail and heard Dara's voice saying she was in London.

Margate was getting old, even though he had only been there a couple of days, and he figured it was not a town you could get lost in. The message from Dara was all the encouragement he needed to go to London.

The men would be watching the stations, waiting for his return. Victoria, Charing Cross, London Bridge. All the main train routes from Margate to London would be impossible, should he chance it and see if he could slip past. So when the train pulled in at Ramsgate and the announcement was to change here for trains to London Waterloo. Ruben didn't think twice about it.

After a quick change at Tonbridge Wells Station, Ruben arrived seven hours later at London Waterloo. Ruben thought the layout of Waterloo Station surprisingly straightforward. One straight area with platforms placed neatly next to each other in numerical order. A large group of people stood looking up at the large black live timetable boards for their train times and platform number. Every once in a while a few people would start running in order to catch their train leaving in three minutes or five minutes or seven minutes, or whatever the announcement said. As Ruben wandered around the station, he noticed a covered set of tracks that seemed disused. Ruben went up to the ticket office and asked the man behind the counter if he knew the history of the disused tracks. The track was, according to the man, the original track for the Eurostar, when it first came into operation, and had been disused for some years.

Ruben wondered how to get a message to Dara to let her know he was in London, to let her know he was safe. He saw a row of pay-phones. How novel. He also noticed that they also took credit cards. He wondered as to their usage now that most people had cell phones, but it was a convenient way to contact Dara without his own phone being traced. He still couldn't risk telling her the address he would be staying at, though, in case anyone was listening in to her phone. As he pondered what to do, Ruben's thoughts drifted to how this adventure all began - a note behind the nozzle of a gas pump. And he had an idea. He wrote the address of his aunt on a piece of paper and put it behind the receiver of one of the payphones. It was a risk to leave it there, but who really used them nowadays, anyway? It was surely a risk worth taking. Then he dialled Dara's number, and left a message:

'Phone 6 where the Eurostar terminated, like at the gas station.'

Ruben wasted no time. He looked around to see if he was being watched, he'd got used to the signs now, before heading off down the escalators onto the London Underground.

People were packed together on the escalator. He soon found out it was the custom to stand on the right and let people walk down on the left. He found out because the tannoy message said so - a constant reminder to stand on the right and walk on the left. And, amazingly, people here obeyed it. Ruben stood still so as not to draw attention to himself by walking down the moving staircase. Here he could be hidden in between two others who also appeared to be travelling incognito Despite the orderly manner in which people followed instructions here, there still seemed to be a constant wave of chaos as folks narrowly missed banging into each other, walking with their heads down not making eye contact. As in Berlin, there were ticket machines as well as the ticket booth. Ruben was now a dab hand at this European travelling life with no cars and only public transport to rely upon, so bought his paper ticket with quick touches to the screen. He stared at the map of the Underground, such a famous image yet like a secret code to be untangled when used for the first time.

'Where are you trying to get to?' came a voice out of nowhere.

The voice made Ruben jump and the paranoia almost came back that he had been caught. However there was something familiar about the tone of the voice, the same as on the train from Ashford. He turned around to see not the man from the Ashford train but someone entirely different, however all mannerisms were almost identical. He had the same unkempt scruffy look, despite wearing a uniform. He had the same manner about him of helpful indifference. Eager to direct tourists and commuters alike to the right place, every word said with the deadpan expression of a man who had said the same words a hundred times before. Ruben observed the man wave his arms around at a young couple with trendy rucksacks on their back, in an attempt to show them which direction they should be going in. At the end of the conversation, the man started to move in one direction, but the woman pulled him in the opposite direction, and he followed her lead.

Now it was Ruben's turn to ask the gatekeeper: 'I want to go to Notting Hill,' said Ruben.

'Well, you want to take the Jubilee line in a northerly direction to Bond Street and change to the Central line going west. See here,' said the man pointing to a point on the board. It all came into focus, there was a silver line and at some point (Bond Street), a red line crossed it marked by a circle. Quite simple really.

Bond Street was a very famous, very expensive street in London. The stuff of films, James Bond, sharp suits and glamour. Ruben was sure he hadn't been followed, and if he had, leading his pursuers on a wild goose chase round the shops of Bond Street seemed like fun. Anyway, he was wide out in the open, so what could they do even if they did spot him?

Arriving out of the station at pavement level, it seemed like Ruben had been transported to the ideal image of England. The hustle and bustle of the Underground and the bland poverty that characterised Margate, seemed to have vanished. People here walked purposefully, but sedately, and there was a sense of calm and civility.

Ruben walked past large glass shopfronts, immaculately presented. Then he came across a curiosity: a very narrow pedestrianised alleyway. Each side of the alleyway were small shop fronts with bay windows jutting out. So small were the shops that you could only fit about three or four people in each before it became full. Each just sold one type of item, almost like a market. Wallets, watches, ties. It was like entering a dream and for a moment Ruben thought he might have gone back in time. It was a bit of England that really was like a costume drama with no set dressing.

At the end of the alleyway. Ruben stepped out onto Piccadilly Circus - a stark contrast to where he had just come from. In front of him was the magnificent *Ritz Hotel*. The stuff of *Jeeves and Wooster,* and *Sherlock Holmes,* of glamour and sophistication. London really was a piece of work, a place you could lose yourself in - in all senses of the phrase. You could be an aristocrat from the 1920s having lunch at the *Ritz,* be in a 1940s spy thriller chasing down the side streets and back alleys or an eccentric in Notting Hill. But most of all, thought Ruben, it was a great place to hide yourself if you happened to be on the run.

Ruben consoled himself with the thought that when all this was over, he'd return with Dara and immerse himself properly in the world of London. But, for now, he needed to get to Notting Hill.

Once again, rising out of the basement of the city after another ride on the Underground, Ruben arrived on the streets of Notting Hill, and was greeted by yet another part of London with its own distinctive character. 'London is many worlds within worlds,' he reflected. The streets were not busy like Piccadilly, but not sparse like Mayfair. There was activity, but it was not overwhelming. Mainly houses, about three stories, with grand steps leading up to the front doors. It was a sunny day, if a little chilly, but people were sitting on the various ledges, enjoying the sun's rays. Various radios playing music, blending together like a symphony.

It was going to be a bright, bright sunshiny day.

He could feel it.

Ruben rang the doorbell of his Aunt's house and instantly heard squeals of delight from inside. The squeals got closer and closer until the door was opened with a burst, and he was greeted by Great Aunt Sally. Her arms opened as wide as her smile, both so warm and friendly and excited.

'Ah Ruben,' she cried, still holding his shoulders in case he should move out of reach. 'Look at you, you really have grown! I could have sworn it was your uncle who walked up to my door.'

Ruben didn't have time to look at her before she was all over him again, dragging him whole bodied into the house.

'Ian, look who it is! Look who it is!'

A young man, about Ruben's age wandered into the corridor from the kitchen.

'This is Ian, my son,' explained Great Aunt Sally. 'He's just moved in for a short while to look after his mum and get a bit of home cooking. Haven't you, Ian? Just until he gets himself back on his feet after he split up from that girl.'

'Mum!'

Sally had only ever referred to Ian's ex as 'that girl' so Ruben never found out her real name.

'Alright?' said Ian.

They were still standing in the hallway when a bell rang.

'That'll be my stew,' said Sally and pushed past the two lads into the kitchen.

Ruben and Ian sat round a large wooden table as Sally served up her colourful creation. It seemed like the most delicious thing Ruben had ever eaten. The warming home cooking was a godsend after days of supermarket sandwiches that tasted of cold whichever flavour you got. He'd never really explored the side of his family with roots in Trinidad, and finally felt like he'd come home.

CHAPTER NINETEEN

Dara's phone rang. She didn't recognise the number. Geoffrey looked at it and said it was a payphone number.

'Don't answer it,' said Geoffrey. 'See if they leave a message. We can trace the number.'

Dara and Geoffrey listened to the message Ruben left on the voicemail:

'Phone 6 where the Eurostar terminated, like at the gas station,'

'I think I know what he means,' said Dara, answering Geoffrey's puzzled look. 'We found the first clue back in the States behind a pump at a gas station, wedged just behind the nozzle. Is there something like that at St Pancras?

'Could be a payphone,' offered up Geoffrey. 'Same motion.' He demonstrated by mimicking picking up an old dial phone.

Dara wasted no time. She grabbed her bag and headed to the door.

Geoffrey followed her. 'Wait a moment,' he said. 'Ruben used the past tense, didn't he?'

'What do you mean?' said Dara.

'*Terminated*,' said Geoffrey. 'He said *terminated* not *terminates*.'

'So where the Eurostar *terminated*?'

'Yes,' said Geoffrey. 'The Eurostar used to terminate at Waterloo station, not St. Pancras. The men following you wouldn't know that. Ruben knew his phone was probably being listened into, and knew also it would be too risky for either of you to be seen at St Pancras. They'll be watching there day and night. But Waterloo isn't used anymore for international trains. The perfect decoy. You didn't tell me your man was so clever?'

'He isn't...wasn't,' replied Dara quietly, as she left the house.

'Be careful,' said Geoffrey. 'And don't use your phone. They will be tracking it.'

Navigating the tube proved not too problematic for Dara. She was getting used to quickly picking up new skills and negotiating different systems. She was surprised by Waterloo station, how nondescript it was. It didn't have the palace-like glamour of St Pancras but if you looked closely, the famed clock and place to meet was still there, high up above and often missed as the inhabitants of the station looked to the floor as they rushed by to their allotted platform. Just one long walkway with platforms numbered in sequence. It made life easy, the payphones were clearly visible and everything was in easy view. That was also the problem, there were no corners to hide in. Dara suddenly felt exposed. What if they had understood what the past tense stood for? What if they were waiting for her?

Dara needn't have worried. The pursuers had indeed tapped into her phone and after searching in vain for the clue, were waiting patiently for Dara to turn up at St Pancras. Meanwhile, back at Waterloo, Dara went over to the 6th phone of the bank of payphones, picked up the receiver and found a folded piece of paper placed between the mouth of the receiver and the holder. It really was that simple. Memorising the address, she got rid of the piece of paper before even thinking about heading to Notting Hill. She knew better now than to keep any information about her person, just in case the worst happened. She first went back to Geoffrey at Highgate. She was unsure how to proceed now she had the address and needed Geoffrey's advice before she finally met up with Ruben.

The next day Ian said he would show Ruben round the local area.

Ruben felt safe in Notting Hill. Sure that all he had to do was wait for Dara to turn up, and then they could go back to Berlin and continue their search for the package. Looking round the local area with Ruben sounded like a great diversion.

'It's mainly antique shops,' Ian said. 'Girls, they like that kind of thing so there's plenty there to look at.'

Ian hadn't quite got the point that Ruben was happily attached and not interested in girls. Ruben's interest, however, in history and all things olde worlde meant he was genuinely interested in looking at the antiques and junk shops.

The Portobello road, where Ian took Ruben, was a mishmash of different coloured shops, and people dressed in bright colours wandering all over the place. Some of the shops had awnings that hung part way over the street, and some did not. There were some market stalls and covered carts selling fruit and veg, coconuts and street food. Ian walked behind two tall thin young ladies in vintage 70s maxi skirts.

'Trustafarians,' Ian muttered with a slight laugh. Then he saw someone he knew. A rosy blond with a huge smile, casually and somewhat clumsily dressed in jeans and oversized T-shirt - an interesting contrast to others on the street whose casual outfits had been carefully put together.

'Still on for tonight, Ian?' the rosy blonde said. 'We'll get 'em in the music round this time.'

Ruben wondered what on earth she was talking about.

Ian turned to Ruben. 'Tuesday is pub quiz night down *The Elgin*,' he said. 'This is Susan. We're on the same team. We was robbed last week by *The Hillbillies*. Susan, this is Ruben.'

Susan greeted Ruben warmly.

'Lovely to meet you, Ruben,' she said. 'Must go. See you later, Ian!'

With that, Susan carried on down the Portobello Road.

Ruben was really none the wiser but nodded his head in familiarity as Susan went on her way, carrying a number of blue plastic bags full of fruit and veg from the market that seemed to be cutting off the circulation to her fingers.

Ruben ducked into almost every shop, fascinated by the knick-knacks and bric-a-brac, while Ian waited patiently outside or just inside the doorway, depending on who was serving. One shop assistant chatted to Ruben for ages, showing him furniture and explaining the era and circumstances as though they weren't merely objects but breathed some kind of life and had individual personalities, shaped by their past. A Georgian chest of drawers made of a mid-brown walnut wood with doric columns at the sides in a darker colour intrigued Ruben greatly. The pronounced grain gave the piece a beautiful pattern. The brass handles, one of which was missing, were made to look like twisted rope and set on an ornate backing of two bows either side and a bird sitting on top. The unknown craftsman who made this, had put a great deal of effort into it. It was an incredible piece of workmanship. It was a pity that a previous owner, in more modern times, decided to make the lower part of the chest of drawers into a cabinet with doors, sticking the bottom drawers together and sawing them in two down the middle. This may have served a purpose at the time, but devalued the piece enormously. What improved it for one person in one era, Ruben thought, was butchery in another.

'You really are oblivious aren't you?' said Ian, as Ruben came out of the shop.

'What do you mean?' replied Ruben.

'Nothing. Never mind. I like hanging out with you. You bring me good luck.'

Ian went back into the shop and asked the shop assistant to join them at the pub that night for the quiz. He exited the shop with a wide grin on his face.

'Well that's us with a full team tonight,' he said. 'Bring it on!'

CHAPTER TWENTY

Later that evening, Ruben experienced a pub quiz for the first time in his life. He, Ian, Susan and a couple of other friends, sat down at a heavy wooden table at *The Elgin*. Ian waited until everyone had sat down before introducing his American cousin.

'So everyone, this is Ruben,' he said. 'My cousin from across the Pond.'

'You didn't tell us you had an exotic visitor,' replied a woman to his left.

'Ruben, this is Cheryl,' said Ian. 'It was an impromptu visit - the best type of visit. Besides, I don't tell you lot everything.' This seemed to stop Cheryl in her tracks and the only reply she could manage was to raise her eyebrows and smile.

Ian continued: 'This is Susan who you met briefly earlier, and this is Mark, solid mate for years, and this is Rahul and Gwen.'

The whole table looked at Ruben as though he was a specimen. They waited for Ruben to say something. Anything at all.

'Pleased to meet you,' came Ruben's meagre reply.

They all looked away and started shuffling about in their seats with a buzz of conversation among themselves discussing what they wanted to drink.

'So who's going to get the drinks in?' said Gwen.

'You are, since you asked,' came Ian's reply.

'I'll go to the bar,' said Rahul in order to get the evening going. 'What do people want?'

'World peace and an equal society,' joked Susan.

'Well we all want that, but this is *The Elgin*. You're looking in the wrong place, love. You're as likely to get that as a decent beer in the *Flower and Firkin*,' said Rahul. 'So that's a dry white then, Susan.'

'I'll have a *Camden Pale Ale*,' said Mark.

'A *Budvar* for me,' said Ian.

'*G and T*, slimline, mind, if they ask, *Sapphire*,' said Gwen.

Rahul turned to Ruben: 'And you?' he said.

Ruben paused for a moment and took a deep breath as though about to address an audience with a momentous speech: 'As I have just landed in this country and I am new to these parts, and have just met you all, I would like to treat you all to something special. A glass of champagne for each of you, so please get a bottle of what you think. It's on me.'

All were staring at Ruben with wide eyes. What a treat! They all started to applaud Ruben, cheering his generosity.

As Rahul got up, he whispered to Ruben: 'I'll order a bottle of *Prosecco*. Lighter on the pocket. They'll never notice the difference.'

'Okay,' whispered Ruben, a bit confused but going along with his new friend's advice. 'And who wants chips?' Ruben said to the group, raising his voice to cut through the applause.

There was another cheer and enthusiastic clapping, especially from Gwen.

'She'll do anything for free food,' joked Ian, elbowing her in the arm.

'Ow.' replied Gwen, slapping him back.

Chips weren't food but perhaps that was the joke. Perhaps Gwen *really* liked chips. Ruben was also surprised at the tactile familiarity of the group with each other, and with him. Not the 'English Reserve' cliché he had imagined. But this friendliness was also unfamiliar to him. It didn't have the urgency of networking or socialising to get something in return that you found in New York or LA, and even the kids in Atlanta seemed more reserved than this, especially with someone new in town.

Mark had gone to help Rahul with the drinks, the two of them bringing them back in relays. Shortly after, one of the bar staff brought over the chips. That was when Ruben realised his mistake. He asked for chips and looked puzzled when some thick French fries arrived instead. A rookie mistake, though seemingly just what everyone wanted. Luckily, Rahul had thought to come back with his kind of chips, bringing back the most unusual flavours of prawn cocktail and cheese and onion. Rahul opened the crisp packets down the side as well as the top to form a sort of bowl. Ruben was fascinated by this ritual but it did make them easier to share.

Just as the quiz was about to begin, the young woman from the shop came in and sat with the group in between Ian and Ruben, introducing herself as Rebecca.

'A full house!' said Cheryl. 'What fun!'

They hadn't thought of a team name for the team yet. Ruben suggested they call themselves *The Elgin Marbles*. Rebecca laughed, though the others seemed to think it was a 'mad idea', but they went with it.

The compere stepped up to a lonely microphone at the side of the room as though taking to the stage. He wore a grey suit and had a combover, thinly disguising his receding hairline. After a couple of silent taps on the microphone, and then a third which made a loud thud, the compere spoke.

'So you all know the rules by now, but here's a reminder. No mobile phones allowed. Anyone seen using them will immediately be disqualified. That's the *whole* team, not just the individual.' There was a 'boo' from somewhere within the depths of the room, audible but unseen. 'This is a test of knowledge,' the compere continued, not how fast we can look things up on *Google*.'

There was a short pause while the compere unravelled the mic wire which had wrapped around his leg. He stuck his leg out and circled it around in an attempt to wind out the cord and then helped it along with his hands.

'Doing the *Shake 'n' Vac* are we?' said Mark to the table, but audible enough for the whole pub to just about hear. A quiet titter of laughter echoed around the room.

The compere regained his composure: 'There are six categories: History, Geography, Music, Culture, Sport and General Knowledge.

'Sounds like all the GCSEs I failed,' said a voice from the table next to them. Another titter passed around the room.

'Quieten down over there,' retorted the compere. 'If you failed then I hope you've got some others on your team or you won't do very well, will you?'

'Ooo . . .'

More laughter from the room.

The compere continued with a new confidence: 'Geography. What was the Turkish capital city Istanbul called?' He repeated the question with different intonation. 'What *was* the Turkish capital called before it was Istanbul called?'

There was an un-silent pause with the audible sounds of whispering and the wind of movement like ghosts in the attic, as the people on each table turned to one another to discuss the answer without the table next to them being able to hear.

The compere rattled off some more questions and each table's occupants excitedly wrote down the answers. Ruben, at first able to show off his knowledge, was disappointed most of the questions were about English popular culture. However, he was vastly appreciated when a question relating to American politics came up that no one knew the answer to.

'William Henry Harrison,' whispered Ruben to the table in a slow pronounced way, savouring the moment.

Overall, *The Elgin Marbles* came fourth. 'A respectable fourth,' said Ian, though Ruben was not impressed by the placing.

The evening continued with people dancing around each other to get to the bar, and dancing once again, drinks held aloft, to take their place back at the table. As the evening wore on, the chat got louder but less memorable, descending into more a mishmash of different sounds and opinions. But everyone seemed to be determined to have a good time. It really wasn't so different from back home, only the weather meant it was cold if you went outside even in summer.

Gwen appeared to be falling asleep at the table.

'Time for us to leave I think, Gwen,' said Rahul. 'I'll get us a cab.' Ruhal dialled a number on his phone. 'Do you have a cab available? *The Elgin*. No, *The Elgin*!' Ruhal shouted louder and louder, until turning to the group and telling them he was going outside.

With that, Rahul left followed by Gwen.

'I think it's time for us too, my American cousin,' said Ian. 'Don't want to keep the old girl up too late.'

Ruben did what he was told, and the two lads left the pub and started their journey home. Not knowing the area meant Ruben had no sense of how long it took. He looked at the row after row of Victorian houses on each street they turned into, with big bay windows and steps up to the front door. There were lights on in most of the windows and he could see snippets of still life as he walked past, only able to capture a moment in his vision. A group of people sat on sofas watching TV, a small party of silhouettes standing, sitting, holding wine glasses. Each image moved past like a zoetrope, even though it was Ruben that was moving and not the pictures.

Eventually one of the houses turned out to be home and Ian, as carefully and as quietly as he possibly could, turned the key on the lock and opened the door. The house was silent and dark. Barely audible was Sally's breathing and the occasional creak that came out of nowhere without reason. Ian went to his room and Ruben settled down on the sofa under the blanket provided for him, and slept throughout the night, deep in thought, his heavy breathing adding to the ghostly noises of the house.

The next morning the whole house was awakened by the ringing of the doorbell. As Ruben was in the living room nearest the door, it woke him first, jolting him out of his dreamland. The sound of the bell sounded so urgent that he didn't hesitate to get up immediately and answer the door.

And standing there, was Dara.

CHAPTER TWENTY-ONE

Ethan's call to Dara for her and Ruben to return to Berlin had been sudden, out of the blue. He'd given Dara the address of the place Ruben was likely staying - it seemed nothing was unknown to Military Intelligence - and off Dara went. Neither she nor Ruben expected such a call, as they thought the Russians were still after them, but Ethan assured them the coast was clear. How? They didn't know, but they expected to find out.

Dara and Ruben waited in the communal airport lounge at Heathrow for their plane home. They considered Berlin their home now, at least for the time being. America seemed a distant memory and their return still a long way off. In fact, returning there was the furthest thing from their minds.

On arrival at *Berlin-Tempelhof*, Ethan's car was there to return Dara and Ruben to their apartment. Whilst the car tried its best to be understated, its slick black exterior and darkened windows meant it stuck out more than a red Lamborghini in a Lidl car park. It was more elongated than other cars, almost like a dignitary's, which in a way it was. You could see people staring as though they thought a President of a small European country would step from the plane and enter it. Dara and Ruben laughed to themselves when they saw Ethan in the back seat of the car, and realised the ride was for them.

As they drove through Berlin to their apartment, no-one took a second look. Ethan came up to the apartment with them. He wanted to look around, talk to them in their home environment where Dara and Ruben would be more relaxed, thinking they might open up more or think of something they had previously missed.

It was getting too inconvenient for Dara and Ruben to remain in London, and not focus on the job at hand. That was the difference between Dara and Ruben and a professional spy, picked from a top university and trained in-house to focus coldly and unhindered by the distractions of their surroundings. These young jackdaws were distracted by the dimmest of bright lights, full of fascination for anything but the task in hand. The double agent had let Ethan know he was getting impatient. He still didn't trust Ethan to take the matter in hand and wanted these youngsters in the middle as a buffer. So, safe or not, Ethan arranged for Dara and Ruben to come back.

'Our agent has promised to be in touch soon,' said Ethan. 'I don't know how or why, but he thinks you should have found him by now. Is there anything you can think of?'

'We go to a bar called *The White Russian*,' said Ruben. 'We always think it might be something to do with that. White Russian could be a code name.'

Ethan's eyebrows looked up. He knew it couldn't be a coincidence. There are no coincidences. Everything has a purpose. 'Tell me more.'

At that moment the familiar tune from the French horn started up.

'That again!' said Dara, irritated. 'I keep hearing this piece, over and over again.'

Dara didn't have any more to tell, but Ruben did: 'It's from Tchaikovsky's *Symphony No. 2*,' he said, relishing the opportunity to impress. 'Also known as *Little Russian*.'

Ethan's mouth dropped open. This was a revelation. 'It can't be?' he cried. 'It must be!'

Dara and Ruben stared at Ethan with a combination of shock and perplexity.

'I'll explain,' said Ethan. The Little Russian was a code name for a double agent, way back in the 60s. He disappeared sometime in the 70s. We assumed he'd returned, or been caught by the Stasi and executed. If it is him, I am astounded he is here at all. Where he has been all these years, where he's been hiding, and how he has not been discovered, nobody knows. There are so many people after him, especially if it was him who took the incriminating telegram. Are you sure there is nothing in the apartment you have found? Anything, however small. He would have left something, even something quite ordinary, that was his style.

After a pause Dara spoke. 'There was this saucer, when we first came, it was broken, we almost threw it away but I thought it looked pretty so I tried to put the pieces together.'

'Saucer? What saucer? What are you talking about?' asked Ethan impatiently. 'Where is it?'

Dara was taken aback by this violent reaction to her innocent, well-meaning remark. She looked at Ruben for comfort and reaction. He looked across at her blankly but calmly, which rubbed off her. Dara composed herself and spoke in a measured manner.

'It was a saucer,' said Ruben, 'as in a cup and saucer. I know it sounds a little out there but it is serious, and in a way rather brilliant.'

'What do you mean?'

Dara continued: 'There was writing on the back. Here I wrote it down'.

Dara pulled out a piece of paper from her purse and showed it to Ethan who dutifully copied it down into a small notebook he pulled from the inside pocket of his jacket, sounding out the letters as he wrote them down.

'*KFOAHFCHTIaAHrT0 (NH)*'

'I mean, who'd think to look underneath a saucer for a lead,' mused Ruben.

'Or who would think of writing it there in the first place,' answered Ethan.

Dara chimed in: 'I wonder if it was meant to be broken or it just fell?'

The two men didn't answer.

'This must be it,' Ethan said. 'I'll get my code breakers onto this.'

Ethan got up: 'You did well. I'll be in touch.' Then he left the building, leaving Ruben and Dara sitting alone in their apartment.

That evening Ruben and Dara decided to go to *The White Russian*.

It seemed so strange to be there without April and Justin. They sat in a booth all by themselves. Maxim didn't come over, so Dara went to the bar to order drinks. Maxim greeted Dara cordially, but not the enthused welcome they usually got when they came in with April and Justin.

'I have not seen you in here for a while,' he said. 'I hope all is well.'

'We went to London for a bit of sightseeing,' said Dara, quickly.

'London, eh?' Maxim nodded his head. When Dara took out her purse ready to order the drinks and pay for them quickly, the paper with the code written on fell out onto the counter. Maxim picked it up, glancing at it.

'Mmm, this is interesting, what is it?' as though he already had an idea.

Dara snatched it back.

'Okay,' replied Maxim casually. 'It's just I wondered what you were doing with Russian writing. You don't speak it do you?'

Dara flicked her head and turned around, drawing closer to Maxim leaning over the bar: 'Russian writing?'

Maxim sighed and said: 'Give me that.' He held out his hand and took the paper from Dara's hand. She looked at him nervously hoping she'd done the right thing and he wasn't going to throw it away. Whilst Maxim studied the paper closely, Dara held her breath but let it out with relief when he started speaking again in a familiar in a chatty tone.

'Look here,' he said, pointing to the letters. Every other letter clearly spells 'Konstant', then 'in' making Konstantin. It was my father's name.' Maxim's informative manner turned into a faraway look as he seemed to return to the world of his childhood. 'Anyway, the others I can't see off hand. Nothing springs to mind. They could be numbers, they use letters for numbers in the Cyrillic alphabet, you know.'

Maxim handed the paper back to Dara and started serving a customer who had been waiting at the bar, then moved on and seemed to forget their conversation. It was strange to Dara that Maxim seemed not to be as intrigued by this, as she was. With a lot to take in she slowly walked back to the table where Ruben sat impatiently.

'What took you so long,' he said. 'And more to the point, where the hell are the drinks?'

'Eh?' said Dara.

'Okay, daydreamer,' said Ruben, getting up to go back to the bar and fetch the drinks. 'I guess it's up to me.'

'No, we should go back to the apartment,' said Dara.

'Why?' replied Ruben. 'I need a drink. I've been looking forward to this all day.'

'I guess I need one too, after what Maxim just told me.'

'What was that?' said Ruben, sitting back down again.

'Get me a red wine first, then I'll tell you.'

'Must be serious, you only drink red wine when you have something important to think about,' replied Ruben, and he went to the bar.

Whilst waiting for Ruben, Dara examined the letters again.

'So what's this all about?' replied Ruben, placing a glass of red carefully in front of Dara, and taking a seat, pint in hand.

'It's the symbols on the saucer, they're letters from the Russian alphabet.'

'How do you know that?'

'Maxim told me,' replied Dara. 'He says they spell out a name.'

'How did he... I won't ask,' said Ruben. 'Let's go home after these. There may be someone listening in.'

The two drank in relative silence talking as though they were on a date they couldn't wait to escape from.

'What did you think of the last Coen Brothers movie,' asked Dara.

'Which one?

'The one in Paris.'

'Yeah, loved it.'

'Me too.'

'What did you think of *The Lady Killers* remake?'

'Don't know, didn't see it, didn't know there was an original.'

'It's a British classic.'

'Why would they remake it?'

'I don't know, the original was so good, even though it was made in the 50s. It was what they call an Ealing Comedy.

'Really? Why do they call it that?' replied Dara, completely disinterested.

'They were made at studios in Ealing.'

'How do you know all this stuff?' replied Dara.

'Okay, I've finished. Let's go,' said Ruben.

When they got up to leave. Maxim was serving customers, but clocked them as they opened the door.

'See you tomorrow,' he said.

'Yeah, see you,' replied Dara, not thinking it strange that he should specify the day he expected to see them again.

So they meandered out of the bar and got the train back to their apartment.

When they got back to the apartment, a postcard had been put through the letterbox, and lay on the floor just inside the door. Dara picked it up. The front of the postcard showed a scene from a James Bond movie.

'Who's that woman coming out of the sea?' said Dara. 'This picture is famous, isn't it?'

Ruben took the postcard. 'It's from *Dr. No*. The actress is Ursula Andress, and she plays Honey Ryder - a clear reference to *The Honey Pot*.'

Dara shook her head, half impressed and half appalled at Ruben's knowledge of trivial things, and took the postcard back off him. When Dara turned the postcard over, she saw there was writing on the back.

'What does it say?' said Ruben.

'*The Devil is forever a Lucky Cat*. Okay. So what does that mean?'

'Even I can work the first bit' replied Ruben.

'What then?' said Dara, challenging him.

'Devil, 666. And, of course, *forever* is infinity, and the symbol for infinity is the same as the number eight,' continued Ruben.

'And luck is 7,' continued Dara. 'Not exactly brain surgery, this. I guess he realised we weren't so bright.'

'What about the cat?'

'Cat's have nine lives,' said Dara. 'So, that's 666 8 7 9'

'That was easy,' remarked Dara. 'They must be getting desperate. What do you think it means?'

'So, we have 666879. Konstantin. This must be a street, or a place or something.

'We need to tell Ethan,' Dara, getting out her phone and dialling his number.

The phone rang only twice before being picked up.

'I need to speak to Ethan,' Dara said urgently.

'Who is calling, please?' came the formal voice of the maid.

'It's Dara!'

'I'm afraid he is not available.'

Dara continued in frustration. 'I must speak to him, it's really important!'

'It's okay,' Dara heard Ethan say to the maid, obviously on another line. 'I'll take this one,'

Dara listened for the click as the maid put her end down.

'What is it, Dara? Has something happened?' Ethan said, calmly.

'It's the code, I've cracked it - *we've* cracked it! It was on a postcard, and-!'

'Don't say any more, I'll be straight round.'

And the phone went dead.

Dara was a bit disappointed that she wasn't given the chance to reveal the code to Ethan there and then.

'He cut me off,' complained Dara.

When Ethan arrived, he took the postcard and put it in his pocket.

'Thank you,' he said.

Dara and Ethan sat there, a little disappointed and a little bemused.

'We need to find the *Little Russian*,' Ethan said. 'Pack some clothes. You're going to Budapest.'

CHAPTER TWENTY-TWO

Dara and Ruben had found Berlin very much like New York - full of young international 20/30 somethings, though unlike New York they were able to take advantage of the cheap accommodation and intense night life. This meant that they were not obliged to immerse themselves in a completely different culture. Standing in Berlin Central Station, looking at the ground, Dara fantasised what Budapest might be like. Even though the dust had long settled on the Eastern Block, it's image of grey, grimy streets still remained.

Ruben was excited to be going. During his visits to the library in Berlin he had started to read up about the Jews and the Gipsies in Hungary during the war. He wanted to see all the places he'd read about, not just during the war but the glory days of the Austro-Hungarian Empire. He wanted to see if the myth of the colourful gypsy culture and grand days of the waltzes and busy cafe society still held true.

Dara wondered with a tinge of foreboding what Budapest might hold for them. The only other thing she knew about Hungary was Dracula was from near there. An avid reader of vampire novels as a teenager, she thought Transylvania had something to do with Hungary but didn't quite know what. Being a city, she didn't imagine she'd find many vampires in Budapest. She wasn't like Ruben who, it seemed to her, was almost fanatical about looking up every piece of history and detail about everything. She was content with wondering and imagining. Though she was recently mildly shocked to discover that Lapland was an actual place. She imagined the land of Dracula, of castles and open spaces. Though in Central Europe, Ruben informed her even cities have their castles.

The glass panels of the station projected squares of light onto the concrete floor and Dara stood firmly inside one of them, as though it would keep her safe. She heard the echoes of voices, creeks, clatters and footsteps. She did not see where they came from as the sounds came from corners she could not see into. Dara and Ruben squinted up at the boards informing the soon to be passengers of the train times and their platforms. There were so many it took her a while to pick Budapest from the menu of cities. Eventually, the destination revealed itself and they made her way to the platform.

The train to Budapest involved a four hour stop off in Vienna - longer than usual due to works on the line. What to do in Vienna for four hours? A guidebook Ruben had bought at the station made a few suggestions. Ruben jumped on '*Eat Sacher-torte at the Sacher hotel cafe*'.

'It's just some chocolate cake,' said Dara.

Ruben referred to the guidebook, and explained it was a secret recipe and that the many imitations did not come close to the real thing.

'It says here it's only available in the one cafe in Vienna,' said Ruben.

Fine, thought Dara, wondering whether she would get to see the art museums, the Freud museum, the gardens around the Hofburg Palace, and other interesting places, or whether Ruben's desire for chocolate cake would dominate the entire stop-over. Then again, they only had four hours. But to see the original *The Kiss* by Klimt in the Belvedere art museum would be really something.

Another time then, she supposed.

It was an odd time of day to travel, mid-morning, on a drizzly Monday - not a day to go anywhere unless you had to. The commuters and day trippers had long gone and the train was sparse but not empty. Dara wondered where those who were sat quietly in the carriages, were going. Most seemed to be sitting alone, in silence. One read a larger-than-life German newspaper - a language still not familiar to Dara. The newspaper covered the man's face and occasionally the paper shook, like a magic trick, as the man readjusted or turned the page. Another passenger stared out of the window looking intently at nothing, for there was nothing to see, and even if something did happen, the man would still only be seeing it through a window - looking but not seeing.

Dara and Ruben sat, with a heavy thud of exhaustion and relief, on a double seat about halfway down the carriage. The commotion made some of the other passengers look up from their world of silent thoughts for a moment before returning to their solitude. It was going to be a long ride, and they soon began to doze.

When the train shuddered to a halt and the lights came on, Dara and Ruben stirred from their slumber, the train going from the tranquil lulling of the train's forward movement and consistent rumble, to suddenly stopping, ushering in the new noises of busy people walking and talking. It took a moment for them to register that they had arrived in Vienna.

Leaving their luggage in the Zurückgelassenes Gepäck (left luggage lockers), they headed for the main city in search of glamour and chocolate cake. When they stepped outside, they found the rain pouring heavily, adding another layer of grey mist to this grey city. There weren't many people around as they walked along the parade by the opera house, each holding an umbrella. It really was raining on their parade. Dara hoped the rain would mean less people at the Sacher cafe. Ruben stopped to look at the grandiose facade of the opera house, in awe of its magnificently, decorated stone.

But Dara ushered him along.

'Our time is short,' she said. 'And I thought you wanted that chocolate cake?'

From the other side of the street, they watched a group of people with oversized umbrellas get turned away from the cafe, but Ruben was ever hopeful. There were only two of them, after all - not a large group.

As they crossed the road and walked up the steps to the cafe, a man greeted them with an amiable sigh. He looked as though he had come from a different time, dressed in a smart waiter's uniform straight from a 1940s classic film. His uniform consisted of smart trousers, a white shirt, a burgundy waistcoat with brass buttons and a box hat with black peak and the words 'Cafe Sacher' written across it.

Ruben wondered why some jobs had uniforms and some didn't, but didn't think it was worth striking up a conversation with Dara about it.

'I am sorry,' the man said. 'But here is a two hour wait. You can purchase a cake in our takeaway booth across the road instead, if you like.'

The man indicated a trailer on the other side of the street.

'Okay, thank you,' replied Dara, a little moodily. They had come all this way in the rain and they couldn't even get in!

Ruben pressed his face up against the window and looked in at the warmth and the glow and the glamour of the chandeliers, and at the people sat at the tables, looking so much at home in their rich attire. Even in the rain, the cafe was full and invited those who could reserve a place, while Ruben could only glance at the world inside. Next time, he thought. Meanwhile, Dara crossed the road and entered the takeaway trailer. It served a purpose - dishing out chocolate cake to the masses - but there was no atmosphere, no grandeur - a complete contrast to the cafe itself. Nevertheless, once inside the trailer, the array of colourful slices of cakes that lay under the glass counter gave it some attraction.

'We'll have two of those,' said Ruben to the woman behind the counter, pointing at the chocolate covered Sucher cake.

'Certainly,' came the woman's reply, in a soft voice. She wore a similar outfit to the man on the door of the cafe, minus the hat. She barely made eye contact with Ruben as she carefully picked up the slices of cake with silver tongs, putting each neatly into a separate paper bag and handing them to Ruben. Dara, who had been standing behind Ruben but at some distance, handed over her credit card to pay. The woman looked confused for a minute, expecting Ruben to pay. She took the card and pushed it into the card machine, before handing it back to Dara.

'Danke,' said Dara, and she and Ruben left the trailer.

The woman answered: 'Bitte schön,' only when the couple had stepped outside.

They headed back to the station and sat on a bench by the platform and listened to the tannoy announcing the various trains and platforms. As they sat, they ate their cake in the least glamorous of settings.

'My god, this is good!' remarked Dara. 'I mean really, really good.'

'Told you,' replied Ruben.

The guidebook was right.

A little piece of heaven on an otherwise dull afternoon.

CHAPTER TWENTY-THREE

Budapest, 1965

Most people are going about their daily business, cheerful and content. This surprises Anne as she thought they would be more tense but the locals didn't have the worries many Westerners have about their jobs which are secure albeit low paid. Sometimes you could forget that fearful and oppressive ambiance which hovered in the air like an invisible cloud above the city. Andrew is careful here, not speeding once and waiting at pedestrian crossings to cross the road. Budapest is a city where the police mean business. Get caught doing anything, and you'll feel lucky to get a fine or a caution.

Andrew and Anne are going to meet a journalist friend at his club. The journalist is a short, thick set man with black curly hair and olive skin. His eyes are slightly bloodshot as though he hasn't slept well for years. However, he has a friendly manner - even if he is a little worn out - and introduces Anne to the others at the table.

The club is not the glamorous building of London gentlemen's clubs or even the hazy workingman's clubs, but a large hut near a jetty on a stretch of the Danube. The hut reminds Anne of childhood trips to British Home Stores in the 1950s and lunch in the canteen. An unfunny affair with Formica-topped tables and no table cloths. People are wearing swimsuits here, and the pace is slow.

'This is Anne, Andrew's partner,' the journalist says, and whispers, 'she is from the UK.'

There are some hushed exclamations: 'Ah, I see,' and 'Not American then?' before the people at the table fall quiet.

There is no room at the table for all those present, so a tall man with brown hair gets up without saying a word and grabs a couple of chairs from another table, the metal legs scraping across the floor of the hut as he drags them over. As other journalists and families gather for the first part of the lunch, the expression on the host's face becomes more serious. There is some quiet whispering among the party around Ann, though Lord knows why they're whispering, as she can't understand them anyway.

As the group clear their plates, some of the women gather them up, along with the knives and forks, and take everything to an area where they are collected by the kitchen staff. The people here are relaxed, chatting amongst themselves as they clear away, a task they have done many times before. The men go outside and select a boat. There is more serious conversation here as they work together to plan a complicated manoeuvre. One man gets onto the boat and two more start to untie it from the jetty. Two other men and a woman pick up large bags holding boxes and food, and hand them to the man on the boat. They have to swing the bags so the man can catch them over the gap of water between the ground and the boat. A woman gets in the boat to help catch the bags and put them in a secure place on the boat.

The tall man who took the chairs, barks something at the woman putting the bags away, and she turns around and says something back. She then picks up a bag and hands it back to him. He looks through the bag and, with a look of relief, hands it back to the woman.

Anne cannot understand what they are saying, but amuses herself by imagining the conversation.

The man: 'What are you doing with that bag?'

The woman: 'I'm putting it on the boat like you asked.'

The man: 'But it hasn't got the cutlery in it.'

The woman: 'Yes it has, I put it in.'

The man: 'Okay, give it to me so I can look.'

The woman: 'You don't believe me, there, take a look.'

The man: 'Okay, it's there.'

The woman: 'Told you.'

The conversation was probably nothing like that, but it was one explanation. Eventually the rest of the party comes out and, one by one, steps onto the boat. There is a more light-hearted atmosphere now as one woman nearly loses her balance and laughs as she just about catches the boat and pulls herself up. Her friends help her sit down and they sit with each other chatting.

Andrew, or Andras as the people here called Anne's fiancé, explained on their way over to Hungary that the communists are suspicious of everything and you never knew who was really a Stalinist. Anne sits listening to the language she does not understand, following its rhythms and melodies as if at a recital. She is cold and needs the loo, and she is swayed around in the wind, Anne does not say anything. She is also hungry - anxious to get stuck into the barbeque to come. The hunger along with the rocking of the boat turns into a feeling of nausea.

Anne rocks around on the boat. She looks at the dusty sandy soil of the bank with sprigs of grass sticking up and a row of very narrow canoes. The boat stops by a jetty, still visible in places but mostly hidden by the grass bank. The party on the boat gets into canoes, five per boat. Anne is shown to the end of one of the canoes. There is no seat or plank of wood to sit on so she sits folded up in the narrow space. This seating position is an apt expression of how she is feeling, curled up on a dark winter's day, except this is daytime and the height of a hot summer. She dares not move in case the canoe topples over. The cold water gives some of its spray to her as the oarsman dips in his oars and rows. She looks up and smiles, after all the English don't complain.

Some minutes later, they reach a small island and alight onto the sandy grass soil. Anne finds a small shrub to sit near, providing some shade and watches the others prepare lunch in the open air. Some go to collect kindling while others arrange a circle of stones. Sticks are found and placed over the stones to create a sort of barbeque. Pieces of speck are arranged on sticks and bread put underneath to catch the hissing raindrops of grease. The whole thing reminds Anne of the time she joined the Girl Guides, hoping to go camping, though the camping never materialised. After relaxing in the shade and eating, Anne feels much better and more like she is on holiday.

Anne has certainly not experienced anything like this before, growing up as she did in Tottenham. The day is exciting to her but overwhelming, but a great end to their visit. She and Andrew need to go to bed early as they set off for their long journey home in the morning.

It is still dark when Anne and Andrew get in the car. They want to miss the traffic and try to get to the border early when the guards might be in a better mood and not tired at the end of a long day.

At the Hungarian border, there are no smiles or welcome greetings, only barbed wire along the sides of the road and numerous watchtowers getting smaller and smaller with the horizon. The border guards stop a grey dirty Trabant two in front of Andrew and Anne. The driver and passengers are hauled out of the car and marched to a hut nearby, and made to wait twenty minutes. They are eventually reunited with their car, and trundle across the border and out of the country.

Anne sees the shadows of soldiers with rifles, occasionally moving, looking, watching for a flicker of light in the surrounding fields and grassland - anything that would betray the presence of a person, moving, creeping, unwittingly reflecting the sunlight or moonlight as they pass a tree. If spotted, the guard would aim his rifle and press the trigger for reasons he could not explain himself, as if a bullet to the torso would place them right back where they came from. Free until they fell into the darkness.

Anne thinks the whole country is a prison.

There is only one car left in front of them, its occupants taken away by the guards without a struggle. Andrew and Anne wait patiently. As twenty minutes ticks by, however, each second getting slower and more filled with dread, their patience starts to wane. Anne looks at her watch.

'Don't do that,' hisses Andrew. 'They might see you and think something's up.'

Anne stares forward, looking nowhere. The guards eventually wave the car in front on. Just like that, the barrier goes up, and the barrier comes down once more, halting Anne and Andrew's journey. A guard comes up to Andrew's side of the car, unsmiling, not an ounce of friendliness in his manner. So different from the warm and friendly folk of the journalist club Andrew introduced Anne to, just yesterday. Another guard comes over to Anne's side, his mannerisms a mirror image of the other guard. It is almost as if they are trained like actors.

Soldiers and guards of the Red Army all over the Eastern block are trained in this specific unwelcoming demeanour, suspicious of foreigners and purposely hostile towards them - a long-standing tradition carried over from Tsarist Russia, then carried over by Lenin.

Andrew is led out of the car into the hut. They'd had to leave the UK in a hurry and Andrew's passport had since expired. This had been rectified at the British Embassy in Frankfurt on the drive across Europe, but the visa was in the old, out of date passport. The two had then been sewn together arousing the suspicions of the guards, desperate to find something.

'What else would it be?' thinks Anne, and more to the point 'Why do they care so much.'

Anne waits in the car for an hour, and still Andrew has not returned. Nothing ever really changes under the surface in places like this, just the colour of the paint.

CHAPTER TWENTY-FOUR

Present day

Dara and Ruben were met at Budapest Keleti station by a man named Istvan. Istvan was a tall, large, kindly man of Turkish descent. There was nothing intimidating about him despite his size and stature. He greeted them with a friendly smile, excited to be of service to these two visitors. He shook Ruben's hand vigorously and gave a customary continental kiss on both cheeks to Dara.

'Hello. Hello,' he said, enthusiastically. 'I am so pleased to meet you and I would be pleased to show you around. If there is anything you need, please don't hesitate to ask me.'

Istvan ordered a taxi which meandered leisurely through the city.

'I'm not really supposed to do this but it seems such a pity to come to this magnificent city without seeing some of it so I've asked the driver to take us on the scenic route,' said Istvan.

Dara and Ruben

Istvan explained: 'Budapest was two cities Buda and Pest. It united into one in 1873 connected by a permanent Chain Bridge, built by the British William Tierney Clark. Many bridges were built soon afterwards. The larger version of the bridge that can be seen at Marlow in the United Kingdom. I've never been but Marlow must be a magnificent town to have such a bridge. Budapest was the fastest growing city in the world like Berlin in the nineteenth century.

Buda is the posh side, hilly green, appealing to the more conservative or middle-aged people looking for a quiet street. It is the castle district built in medieval times, town houses with baroque façade and the huge former Royal Palace. But Pest is where the action is. Theatres, an opera house, concert halls, universities, orchestras, rock bands, clubs, nightclubs, shops, patisseries – café society. Also synagogues, cinemas, grand and beautiful churches, the works, it's all there. Beautifully built block of flats in Italian renaissance, baroque styles. Also, later central European art nuevo and art deco. Pest is flat but there are magnificent views on the river side toward Buda and the Royal Palace.

The taxi stopped at the castle which looked down on the river Danube. Dara and Ruben got out of the taxi and wandered along the open turrets, looking through the gaps in the stone, down at the river below and the parliament building opposite. Above was the decorative angles, spikes and towers of St Stephen's church. There was a sense of tranquillity about the place and at the chance to be tourists for just a moment. The peace was gently disturbed by Istvan who, following at a respectful distance, gently reminded them that they needed to get on.

'We need to get on,' he said. 'I hope one day you will return as a tourist but for now we must have another mission in mind.'

Istvan lead them to a subway station and they embarked a couple of stops outside the main city centre on the Pest side. Emerging onto ground level, they were greeted by a very different site. Gone was the glamorous and ancient city, instead, rows of concrete tower blocks where people lived, designed to be practical and server.

Istvan took Dara and Ruben to one of the tower blocks, though it was difficult to tell which one as they all looked alike. They crossed the mosaic floor in the lobby that said 1967 in a circle, then were led into a small lift with manual iron doors that pulled across like a gate. Up they went, squeezed together in a small space the size of a wardrobe, except they weren't going to Narnia. The lift took them all the way to the top floor, spilling them out into a dimly lit narrow corridor with dark green carpet and dark brown walls. The few doors had long windows in the middle of them, fronted with iron bars.

Istvan removed some keys from his jacket pocket and casually opened a door to the right of the lift, ushering Dara and Ruben inside the apartment before following them in and closing the door carefully behind him.

The place was eerily quiet. It seemed no-one else lived in the entire building, even though an occasional whistle of a kettle or a dull thud could be heard. But these seemed more like the activity of ghosts than humans going about their daily business.

Dara and Ruben were shown into the living room by Istvan. The furniture was like something out of an elderly person's condo in Florida from the 1970s. There wasn't anything after 1980 to be seen. Dara walked up to a brown bookshelf and started looking through the books.

'Hey, Ruben,' she said, beckoning to Ruben. 'There's German books here, and some in English. And I guess this must be Hungarian right?'

Ruben wandered over to where Dara was standing.

'Amazing,' sighed Ruben, looking at some of the larger books on art, taking them off the shelves to see what was inside.

Dara wandered into the bedroom, and over to a nondescript bed with a flowery towelling bedspread. No headboard or anything to betray its age.

The partition between the bedroom and the living room was open and Dara noticed that at the other end some glass doors opened onto a tiny balcony. She marched over there and stood in awe at the panoramic view of Budapest.

'Ruben,' she exclaimed. 'Take a look at this, this is awesome.'

Ruben put the book he was looking at back on the bookcase, and joined Dara to look at the view. Beyond the tops of 60s tower blocks, far on the horizon, loomed a set of shadowy hills.

'That's the Buda hills,' said Istvan, looking intently out at them for some time before returning his gaze to the flat.

So fascinated were they by the view, Ruben and Dara didn't yet notice the closed door in the entrance hall. So when Istvan said: 'Anne, you can come in now', they were a little startled.

A lady in her sixties opened the door and came in from what was a small kitchen to the right of the hallway.

'Maggie?' squealed Dara.

'I am sorry to startle you,' Maggie said. 'This must be a surprise for you.'

'What are you doing here? Why aren't you in London? What the hell's going on? Where's Geoffrey?'

'Geoffrey is fine. He's back in London, holding the fort.'

'So why are you here?' said Dara.

'I've been here before,' said Maggie, 'in my younger days. I had a Hungarian lover who came over in the fifties with his family and we went to visit them. I was called Anne then. I went by my middle name - Maggie - when I got back to England in order to keep a low profile.'

'That's all very interesting,' Ruben said, 'but why are *we* here?'

'I need to show you something,' replied Maggie.

Maggie, Dara and Ruben travelled up the Danube on a tourist boat. A very different affair to Maggie's last experience. There was a tour guide, for a start. Germans and a few English chattered away. The boat crew nattered away on the tannoy system, each taking their turn to inform the passengers of timings and the historic buildings on either side of the river. Then a special announcement: *'And don't forget we will be stopping at an Island for a real traditional Hungarian BBQ. Relax and enjoy the air.'*

There was a proper jetty where the tourist boat could dock, allowing the passengers to alight with ease. A stone BBQ was laid out on the island, still rustic by American standards, but robust enough to be used on a daily basis. There were picnic tables and plates and cutlery, and a hut in case it rained.

As the rest of the party milled about and the crew set up the camp stove to cook the food, Maggie sneaked off, followed by Dara and Ruben.

Maggie looked around the clearing on the island where she had sat so many years before, though it could have been last week, she remembered it so clearly.

Most of it, anyway.

'Where was it again?' Maggie thought, looking around desperately.

She saw a section where the grass grew taller than its neighbouring plots which seemed familiar. She dug down into the damp earth with a spoon she had retrieved from the catering team. But this was not right. The tall grass had been a landmark but not the actual spot. It was somewhere nearby, though.

Maggie moved a few feet to her right, and started digging in a patch of bare earth mixed with sand from the banks of the river. Not there, either. But near. Eventually, she found a stone, unassuming and yet slightly different to the rest - grey with black and rust coloured streaks. On close inspection, she found it had a hole in the middle and a small pebble pushed through.

This was it.

Maggie dug down frantically with the spoon. It must have looked unconvincing to anyone watching. How far could you get with a spoon anyway? But what she was looking for wasn't buried deep. Maggie pulled from the ground a small metal box. Inside was a cassette tape and an old black and white photograph of a man. On the tape was written *Tchaikovsky's Symphony No. 2*.

CHAPTER TWENTY-FIVE

Seventeen hours on the night train from Budapest to Berlin had left them absolutely exhausted. As soon as they got back to the apartment, Ruben collapsed onto the sofa and Dara threw herself onto the bed. But not without a sense of achievement. They had the recording of Tchaikovsky's *Symphony No. 2*, along with a black and white photo of the man who must surely *be* the Little Russian - their elusive contact. It seemed obvious, but then this wasn't a game. If it was a game, it was a game of wits for the witless. For years, The Little Russian didn't want to get caught so he left no clues to solve, until he wanted to be found, then it was a game where identities and information needed to be hidden but easily discovered, with no ambiguity. Ambiguity leads to misunderstandings and costs lives.

One thing bugged Dara. Why would someone in hiding so long ago arrange the future discovery of their identity? In those days, you never knew what was going to happen, Dara thought. If there was a mistake on one side, you needed to be able to prove without doubt who you actually were. It made sense. You couldn't take any chances. The music plus the picture was the proof of the Little Russian's identity.

Just look at the collapse of the Berlin Wall, as quickly as it had gone up. Overnight. Poor old Chris Gueffroy, or should that be poor *young* Chris Gueffroy. Just out of his teens, his whole life ahead of him, Chris could stand it on the East side no longer. With the confidence of youth, he tried his luck - and failed - becoming the last person to be shot attempting to cross the wall. Nine months later, the time it takes for a woman to come full-term and breathe life into the world, Chris would have got his wish without his breath of life vanishing into the air.

A month later, Winfried Freudenberg flew too high in his balloon over the wall, crashing to the ground a few hours later and becoming the last person to die attempting to cross. These were not near misses, they were near *survivals.* No one ever talks about that. Those who died but almost survived, in the pursuit of trying to live the life others were simply born to.

Sat on their familiar balcony looking at the stars, Dara and Ruben wondered what was expected of them now. What were they supposed to do next? What was supposed to happen? No-one had heard from April, or Justin for that matter, so they guessed working at *The Honey Pot* was not something they would be doing. They could live on rice and lentils for a while, they guessed, perhaps ask Ethan for some funds. They were due to meet Ethan tomorrow to hand over the photo and the tape, so perhaps they could ask him then.

The familiar music started up again. But this time Ruben and Dara knew exactly what it meant. The music, the postcard. He was here, in the building. But where? All the apartments in the block had been accounted for, although, as Justin once told Ruben, it wasn't unusual for a secret room, basement, attic, to be hidden away behind a cupboard in these places, though. That's what Justin had told Ruben once.

They decided to follow the sound of the French horn. The music seemed to get nearer then further away, leading them to a cupboard. Could this be the one? They moved the cupboard and found a door. Yes, this must be it. But when they opened the door, all they found was another cupboard. Why would you put a piece of furniture in front of an in-built cupboard? The music suddenly changed from the now familiar tune to another one, the theme to *James Bond.* Remembering the postcard with that scene with Ursula Andress as Honey Ryder, Ruben saw it as a message to open up *The Honey Pot.*

After dropping the postcard and the tape to a very excited Ethan early the following day, Dara and Ruben made their way to the cafe.

The pair opened up *The Honey Pot*, dusted off the tables and prepared for the day. Luckily, it was a quiet day as even the regulars assumed it was closed for good, so long had it been shut. Dara and Ruben sat around, served the few customers that came in and waited for something to happen.

But nothing did.

All day Dara mulled over the significance of the words on the postcard, and the code on the saucer. Maxim told her the letters were Cyrillic and that Konstantin was clearly visible to anyone who spoke Russian. Was Konstantin a person? If so, who?

Perhaps there was a street named Konstantin? Dara and Ruben went to the library the next day, instead of opening up *The Honey Pot*, and tracked down a large street map book of large German cities. There was not a Konstantinstrasse in Berlin, but there was in Leipzig, Frankfurt, Munich and Bonn. 'Not more travelling,' Dara thought. She was sick of trains, planes and cell phones. There really was only one way to find the answer, and that was to do it the old-fashioned way, sifting through the telephone directory looking for businesses on Konstantinstrasses in Germany to see if perhaps there might be something that might have a safety deposit box.

Maxim gave them an old telephone book from a shelf behind the bar at *The White Russian* - planted there a long time ago. So, off they went, sat in the cafe, looking up each building in each street named Konstantin. 'I think I've got it,' she said to Ruben.

'Where?

'I've found one in Frankfurt, this place here.' Dara pointed to the description of the business. 'It says printers and post deposit,' Dara continued. 'What else could it be?'

It wasn't certain, but it was the only thing that stood out among the various Konstantinstrasses. She had nothing else. It was more than worth a shot.

The scenario of getting off a train and walking along unfamiliar streets had become so familiar to Dara and

Ruben, they didn't even think about it. Streets are very much the same wherever you go. There are buildings with a road down the middle where cars go up and down - sometimes trams or buses - and people walking either side. At a glance, even the people look the same. Same hair styles, same clothes, same manner of walking to and from work, shopping, going to lunch. The same routine throughout most of the world. It is only when you look closely do you see the subtle differences, each nationality desperately trying to hold onto their traditions developed over years of separation.

Dara and Ruben stepped into the little printing shop. The grey carpet had not been cleaned for some time. There was a large printing machine in the middle purring away at regular beats, the heart of the operation, and a bank of safety deposit boxes set through an opening with no door, into the rear wall. A few people queued at the printer, printing business reports, 'to be copied 100 times and bound,' and so on.

Dara and Ruben edged past the printer and made their way to the back of the shop.

'Where shall we start?' said Ruben.

But Dara was already tapping the code into the first box.

'Try them all, she said. It has to be one of these.'

'Click', said the first post box. But it didn't open. Dara tried the next one, but it wasn't right either. She tried them all, without success. Ruben and Dara looked at each other.

'What the fuck?' said Ruben.

'Don't look at me,' replied Dara. I'm the one who's done all the workings out,'

'Right, so where did we go wrong,' said Ruben, shifting into a calmer, matter of fact voice. 'Did you actually transcribe the numbers in the clue,'

'No,' replied Dara in shame. 'I mean what else can it be, the number for the Devil 666, infinity - 8, lucky 7 and cats - 9?'

At that moment they became aware of someone standing in the shadows of a doorway which led from the public part of the shop to some sort of storeroom. The man was short, with a shaved head and uneven skin. Ruben instantly recognised him as the guy behind the bar that very first evening at *The White Russian*, and if he looked closely enough, he bore a startling resemblance to the man in the black and white photo.

'You have it wrong. The number of the Devil is 616,' the man said in a slow, deadpan voice. 'Not 666.'

Dara and Ruben stared dumbfounded, as frozen as a pair of Pompeii figures playing a game of *Grandmother's Footsteps*.

'You're the...' Ruben said, but he didn't get to finish the sentence before Dara cut in.

'Why here?' she said to the Little Russian, 'And why has this taken so long? You knew where we were in Berlin, you could have just given us the telegram.'

'You think I chose this life?' said the Little Russian, his voice cracking with emotion. 'Everyone is after me. Everyone has always been after me. I didn't want to do it in the first place. I just got caught up in the whole drama. I lived the quiet life in Leningrad. Simple clerical job, no-one to bother me. But then I had access to some papers, some documents. They wanted me to take them, to see what was in those files. After that, you name it, they wanted me to pass on the information. You don't say no to these people.'

'Who are *they*?' asked Dara.

'Everybody and anybody. KGB, Russian Mafia, the Kremlin, all trying to get one up on each other whilst trying to get one over on the West. No-one ever thinks of the little man in the middle. I guess at first I was flattered to be asked. Little me having the big shots noticing me, not ignoring me or kicking me down. They were welcoming and charming. I felt I had friends, like I was *somebody*. They gave me the code name 'Little Russian'. But then things got complicated.'

As Dara and the Little Russian spoke, Ruben began trying the safety deposit boxes with the new code.

The Little Russian continued: 'The mafia found out about the telegram, the one implicating a US President's failed liaison with the USSR, the one the Kremlin had on file. They wanted it to blackmail the US, and the KGB wanted it to destabilise the West, show them who was the best. But they didn't understand, no-one cares if a President from way back then was corrupt. *Every* president is corrupt. In *every* country. The little man, if he is corrupt or a criminal, then they put you in jail to rot. They put you in jail for the slightest of things. If you step on the cracks in the pavement, even by accident, because when you do, you rock the fragile ground underneath. But the leaders, the higher ranks, they commit the worst kinds of crime. You never see them struggling for food.'

Dara heard Ruben swearing under his breath behind her, as he continued to punch the numbers. But the Little Russian was in full flow. It was as if the words he was saying had been chained up inside him for years.

'*Perestroika* and *Glasnost*, they changed nothing. We are still dictated to and we are still poor. The people at the top still live in ivory towers, untouched by day to day troubles. They make their decisions with no sight in their eyes or sounds in their ears of those who bear the consequences. You may vote in President after President in your country, but what are the changes? There are still poor and rich, and you have people living on the streets, people without jobs. At least no-one in Russia calls the street a home, or finds themselves with no income all of a sudden, with bills to pay. Even if our apartments are small, even if our jobs are tedious, even if we have to queue for bread, at least we know we have a home and a job to go to, not in the West.

'So why are you working for us then?' interjected Ruben, nearing the end of the second row of boxes.

'An Englishman, a true British gentleman. That is the reason. There were a few in the old days. None now. They liked our ways in the Eastern block and didn't see the cracks, they were not looking. Some of them turned double

169

agent and worked for the KGB. They saw we had the evidence - the telegram. One of them turned back. He turned not because he longed for the past but because he wanted the truth to be known. He did not turn into a pillar of salt. His desire was infectious. He showed how we should be. So I looked for the telegram myself. Then the CIA got wind, through another double agent, I suppose. There were so many, it was hard to tell whose side anyone was on. If anyone was on a side at all. Their own side? Not even that. We are so easily persuaded to join one side or another and there is some comfort in loyalty.'

'Weren't you scared?' said Dara.

'They promised me a better life, so no, I was not scared. In Russia, there is no glittering golden carrot at the end of the road. No promise of riches, however foolish the glitter is that blows away in the wind. You spend time waiting for cake, when you could get another almost the same in the shop next door. You only have to dream, keep on dreaming until the dream runs out, and you seep into your final rest into the air. But you can be kept alive. By the 1960s the illusion of Communism and the destruction of Stalin's regime took its toll. It was a sinking ship kept afloat by hot air, not the concrete we saw above the surface.

I have guns pointing at my head from all sides. Whatever I do, one of them will pull the trigger. They need to take action so others can see, even if the action they take makes no sense, it is the action that makes the hero. They will shoot into the air but the bullet will find its way to me. I've been hiding all these years. Watching, waiting. To see if the promise of this new life will be kept, to see if the new life is the promise that exists. I had to be sure it would be true. I trusted no-one.'

Dara turned from the Little Russian to Ruben, and asked him how he was doing.

'Last row,' he replied.

'It was no life to live,' the Little Russian continued. 'In a revolving room hidden behind a cupboard, in the basement of an apartment block in Berlin. That is no life at all. The room moves from one side to the other to receive goods from the street side and then to the storeroom with another cupboard where I would hand things on. But I didn't want to keep on moving whilst staying in one spot. At least a prison cell has a window in which to see the light.

I needed to finish what was started but I couldn't trust anyone in the surrounding world. They do not mean well. I needed some innocents to cut through the trust. Someone with no agenda. To act as go-between, to deliver and to speak on my behalf. To show if the life they pledged would be assured.

'So that's where we came in?' suggested Dara.

'I have a cousin, Konstantin, in Budapest. His father - a journalist -stayed after liberating the city from the clutches of Nazism, having fallen in love with a local girl. He remembered an American woman, the girlfriend of a refugee. He took them out for the day. We had planned my disappearance, I didn't do this all alone.

It was on this day that Konstantin had chosen to bury my identity. We always do this in case we disappear. We don't leave clues to solve because we don't want to be caught. So we bury our identity where X marks the spot, no riddles to solve, there might not be time. We did not know we would have guests that day - Andrew and Anne - but in some ways it was the perfect opportunity. This way we had someone on each side of the fence who could prove my worth. We, Konstantin and I, thought it a good place to start. It was easy really.'

'Got it,' cried Ruben, and turned round with a small package in his hand. But it was as if the Little Russian was more interested in his telling of the story than the actual story unfolding around them.

'We could see you coming, across the horizon. There was no-one else around. Like myself, the mundane existence we all face year after year, waiting for something to happen., was the life you lived.'

'But how did you know?' said Dara.

It was as if the Little Russian didn't even hear.

'Usually our hopes are in vain but when we are desperate, when the glimmer of hope appears, it is like a feast. We grab the low hanging fruit presented to us. Life does bring us wonderful adventures after all. Even if you didn't bite, someone would eventually. But you did and here we are. You often did not see the clues, but then you are not trained in espionage. I did not account for this at first. But I have now revealed myself to you once more, to help you on your way. To take the piece of paper to -'

The Little Russian didn't finish his sentence. After hearing a gentle thud, Dara watched as he slid to the floor, as if every muscle in his body had failed him at once. A nondescript man walked away quickly, losing himself in the crowded street.

Ruben and Dara fled the shop in panic. But all was normal on the Konstantin Strasse. They ran back inside, wanting to see if the old spy was okay, expecting a huge commotion over the discovery of his body. But all was normal in the shop too.

The Little Russian was nowhere to be seen.

CHAPTER TWENTY-SIX

Dara had the telegram in her bag. Time had passed and it was now a dark and cold autumn evening in Frankfurt as they wandered to *Weisser Stein* subway station. No car had been organised by Ethan, or taxi, which was a little disappointing. They passed the desolate, lifeless *Nordwestzentrum* shopping mall - empty even though it was still open.

Ruben looked at the map.

'We've walked the wrong way,' he said, turning around.

Dara reluctantly followed without saying a word. They walked through the side streets now damp with rain. A man walked past them too close and knocked Dara on the shoulder. It was purposeful, meaning to intimidate or even gain an advantage and run off with what he could. But Dara held her bag with both hands, fully aware of its precious cargo. None of the common thieves lurking in these side streets would succeed, if she could help it. And if they did, they might be getting more than they bargained for.

Walking past the *Batschkapp*, there was a sudden rush of people coming out from the building. Wearing dark clothes, they sank into the shadows, making Ruben and Dara wary and on edge. But they soon saw they were just young revellers spilling out onto the street after a *Dead Kennedys* gig, and meant no harm.

Dara smiled to herself. She'd seen the *Dead Kennedys* back home a few times.

Something familiar.

There was almost an hour wait in the dark and cold for the train back to Berlin. Dara and Ruben sat on the bench, looking at the cafes, now closed for the evening. They were both famished - too late to witness the buzz of commuters travelling to Germany's banking district. And too late to get a bite of something to eat.

So long did they wait, that when the train came to take them to Berlin, to home, to comfort, they barely registered it. They got on the cold, dimly lit train in the same despondent manner as they had sat waiting for it. There was a spooky silence on board, and the few people, silent and scattered, around the carriage seemed like ghosts. There was a sense that one could be the monster, the one who would haunt them, pounce on them, and grab the documents they were guarding. Both Ruben and Dara kept watch, waiting to respond to any encounter.

Reaching Berlin just over four hours later, their mood lightened slightly with the more familiar surroundings. There were more people around, stepping off the numerous other trains travelling into this central point. In the streets, people staggered out of bars in ones and twos, and sometimes in threes. A man lost his balance as he walked down the steps of a bar and fell into Ruben and Dara. There was a tense moment as Ruben got ready to confront the stranger, who was possibly trying to grab Dara's bag but after a jumbled apology. It was evident he was inebriated and meant no actual harm. A group of young ladies stumbled down the road, clinging onto each other so as to stay together and not fall down. They laughed as one stumbled, their arms reaching out into the emptiness, thinking the air would catch them if they fell. They did not notice a man quietly walking past and dipping his hand into the coat pocket of one of the women. Dara didn't react, not wanting to attract attention to herself, and pulled Ruben away from this chancer thief.

They didn't want to take any more chances, so Ruben phoned Ethan to arrange a meet. But there was no answer from his cell phone. He tried the landline. The maid answered.

'Ethan and Emilia are not at home,' said the maid in an irritated cut glass accent. 'I was about to leave for the evening, but I will write a note that you called.'

It seemed to Dara and Ruben that the silence and the desolation was spreading.

'I guess we should just go home.' said Dara

'Where will we keep it? It isn't safe there,' replied Ruben.

'What else can we do?'

'We can't even ask Justin to put it in the safe at *The Honey Pot.*'

'Not after what I've seen him do,' said Dara. 'We can't trust anyone. We'll work something out when we get back. It's all we can do.'

'I would never have guessed Justin would be up to something,' mused Ruben.

'He certainly has a lot of explaining to do and I'm going to get it out of him.'

At the apartment, it was difficult to know where to put the telegram as there wasn't an obvious hiding place. If it was obvious, it wouldn't be a good hiding place. They eventually decided to put it in the drawer of a small table that stood, unassuming and ignored, in the lounge. Not even the Russians, who, it seemed, had regularly ransacked their apartment while they were away, would bother to look there. Like people, some pieces of furniture are just not seen by others as important.

Hiding in plain sight, so to speak.

There was a knock on the door. Ruben and Dara, suddenly became very tense.

'Who could it be at this hour?' whispered Dara.

'Should we pretend we aren't in?' said Ruben.

'No!' hissed Dara. 'Just stay still.'

But for reasons known only to himself, Ruben slowly and ceremoniously walked towards the door and carefully pulled the handle down. Gingerly opening the door, he saw the figures of Ethan and Emilia standing there. Relieved, Ruben threw the door wide open and greeted them with a smile.

'Ruben, great to see you,' said Ethan in a commanding voice as he entered the room and sat down on the sofa. I believe you have something for me?'

Neither Dara or Ruben replied.

It is easy for a person to overlook the least noteworthy in the room, those who don't put themselves on display. And sometimes it is these seemingly innocuous, invisible, seemingly unimportant people who are the most crucial. Emilia wasn't one of those, she observed even the loneliest of souls, hidden in the shadows of the sunlight. So transfixed were Dara and Ruben with Ethan, they failed to notice Emilia surreptitiously opening drawers and looking into cupboards, including the little, unassuming table.

'This is what we are looking for,' she said, standing by the open drawer and holding aloft the telegram. 'You have found it for us,'

'But we're supposed to take it back to America,' said Ruben. 'That was the deal.'

'That won't be necessary now,' said Ethan. 'Don't worry, you'll still get paid your 'courier fee' if that's what you're worried about.'

'I'm worried about a lot more than that' replied Dara. 'How did you know we even had it?'

Ethan didn't answer.

'You've done a great job,' continued Ethan as though reading from a script. 'Your country will be proud.'

Emilia handed Ethan the telegram.

As Ethan took the telegram, he said: 'But we can't take any more chances.'

Holding the telegram over the bin by the side of the sofa, Ethan took out a cigarette lighter, pulled the trigger to produce the flame and set the telegram alight. In a single moment, the telegram was dust.

Dara and Ruben were speechless.

Then Dara cried out, 'What the hell did you do that for?' It seemed pathetic and childish, but it was the only thing she could think of saying.

'It is better this way,' answered Ethan. We wouldn't want it getting into the wrong hands again, would we? Like your friend Justin.'

'He's no friend of ours,' replied Dara, trying to salvage something of her relationship with Ethan and Emilia. Not anymore.'

'That's good to hear,' said Ethan. 'Come, Emilia. We must be going.'

Ethan and Emilia casually walked out of the apartment into their night, their steps in unison, as though never to be seen again.

Dara and Ruben were left wondering if what had just happened was a mirage. It was unbelievable, but here they were, the document to take back to the states - the thing they'd been hunting all this time - no more.

'Perhaps it's a good thing,' said Ruben.

'Maybe,' replied Dara 'I hope we're out of it now.'

'Do we just go home?' asked Ruben.

'I guess,' answered Dara. 'But not before I see Justin. I need to know what this is all about.'

CHAPTER TWENTY-SEVEN

Justin was sitting at one end of the café when Dara and Ruben arrived. He immediately knew something was amiss and did not greet them warmly, choosing to stay silent. Dara walked slowly across to him, anger seeping out through the corners of her mouth and eyes.

Ruben tried to follow her but Dara waved him away.

'I need to do this alone,' she whispered. I don't want him frightened off and shut down. It will be too intimidating, I want him to open up, spill, say what he needs to say without interference.'

'But I'm not leaving you alone,' replied Ruben. 'What if he tries something? You just never know what people are going to do.'

'Wait by the door then, if you must,' replied Dara. 'But keep a low profile.'

'Fine,' answered Ruben indignantly. 'But don't you worry, I'll be on hand at a moment's notice. I'll be watching him.'

Justin followed Dara's movements with his gaze. Intimidated at first but then straightened himself up as if getting ready for battle.

'I saw you in London,' Dara said, walking slowly towards Justin, fixing Justin in her sights.

'Where?' replied Justin, genuinely perplexed. Perhaps she was bluffing.

'At the gig. I was there too. You didn't see me, but I saw you,' answered Dara. 'You were talking to a man and then handed something over to him. What was it, tell me!'

'How did you know where to go?' replied Justin, getting more angry at these disclosures. How could he have been so stupid? How was this even happening?

'I saw you in the street in Berlin, hiding in an alleyway talking to someone on the phone. I had gone to meet a friend and was on my way back to the pub to meet you guys. I knew something wasn't right, I mean, why would you be hiding? So I listened. And I was right. The man who had come into the café when I was there with April, the man who spooked her so much, that was the man you were arranging to meet in London. There was something you weren't telling us, wasn't there? And whatever it was, you were keeping it from April as well.'

'You don't understand what's happening,' Justin replied. 'You make judgements without realising which side you are on.'

'What makes you so sure of yourself?' replied Dara, defensively.

'Really!' cried Justin. 'Are you seriously asking me that question?'

Dara didn't know what to say.

'You must understand. Any one of the others, they are all playing political games with you both. You are being used as pawns by all of them. They don't care what's right.'

'It's of national importance to us Americans. We are doing what is right for our country.'

'When did you become so patriotic?' cried Justin in disbelief. 'Your president almost caused a war to end all wars. He almost blew up the whole world!'

'Of course I'm patriotic. Everyone is,' continued Dara. 'But I know our country isn't perfect. Far from it. There is so much wrong that needs to be made right.'

'You don't say?' replied Justin sarcastically. 'I'm on the same page as your words, but not your actions.'

Really,' replied Dara in a softer tone. 'Are you sure about that? I lived as an outsider all my life, an alternative, or so I thought. But I never *did* anything, never made a difference. Not like now.'

Justin continued on his train of thought: 'We strive to make a difference, sitting on the outside, don't we, Dara? But it never comes. We must continue nonetheless, otherwise what's the point?'

'There is always a point,' said Dara.

'If word gets out about this telegram, it will cause mayhem,' Justin said.

'If you don't like war, Justin, don't tempt fate. This is about protection. It is about *preventing* another war.'

'Don't be so stupid, Dara! We are always at war. Where is the outspoken person, the truth seeker I thought you were, Dara? The people deserve to know. It is our duty to expose the truth.'

'The truth won't set you free, Justin. And why should I believe you? You lied to April.'

Justin stopped for a moment. He sighed as his gaze went from Dara to the floor.

'I know,' he said quietly, before speaking more defiantly. 'It was for the greater good.'

'Like killing anyone who got in the way?'

'I've never killed anyone!'

'Not even the Little Russian?

Justin looked up, surprised and sad at the same time.

'Do you mean he's dead?' Justin looked as if he was about to cry.

'He went down. We had to leave him. Probably a poison jab. We think they took him, So, yes, he most likely is dead,' said Dara.

'Ah, that poor little man,' muttered Justin.

Dara returned the conversation to the subject at hand. She wanted to get Justin to confess. Perhaps confess was the wrong word, he'd already done that. She wanted to find out why he wanted to unleash such chaos. But he had explained why. It was a different kind of 'why', it was 'why did he think he was doing the right thing'?'

'Out of destruction,' Justin said. 'Comes a new beginning. A chance to start again. A chance for things to change.'

Then, out of the shadows, April appeared. Dara was so relieved to see her again after all this time. She ran up to her and flung her arms around April in an uncharacteristic display of affection.

'April, I can't believe it's you,' cried Dara. 'Where have you been? I've been so worried.'

April was shy to respond fully but acknowledged her friend's affection by saying warmly: 'Yes, it is me Dara, I am here.'

Justin appeared a little shocked, but did not get up to greet his wife.

April bent down behind the bar and opened the safe, and came up holding a small metal box.

'I'll take this,' she said.

Dara stared, unmoving, waiting for April's next move. By the time Dara and Ruben realised she wasn't taking them with her, it was too late. Both looked at each other in disbelief at their own naivety, both thinking April was on their side.

'What the hell?' said Dara. 'What's in that box?'

'Oh god, you two really are the . . . ' said Justin, stopping himself before he had the chance to finish his sentence and possibly say something insulting.

'The telegram?' cried Ruben. 'But we saw it being burned.'

'Destroyed?' said Justin with a half-smile.

'Ethan burned it in front of us,' remarked Ruben.

Justin mused: 'US Military Intelligence? Now there's an oxymoron.'

'There's two telegrams?' added Dara.

'Fine, I'll explain,' continued Justin. 'I do like you both, despite everything. You mean well.'

'The Little Russian made a copy, insurance so to speak. You never know what's going to happen in this line.'

Dara and Ruben didn't say anything but looked sheepishly down at the floor.

Justin continued: 'In case he got discovered by the other side and his life was in danger. Best to have a back-up. The one you took from the safety deposit box in Frankfurt, that was the copy.'

'So where did you get that one from, the one you have, or rather April has now?' asked Ruben.

'From the Little Russian. He had it in his hands, he gave it to me.'

'How?' asked Dara. 'Were you there too?'

'I followed you to the printing shop. I wondered if the Little Russian would be there waiting for you. I needed to find out who he was, where he was. I just wanted to protect him, I swear. When I saw him collapse, I dragged his body out the back. That's why you didn't see him. He had the original on him. He took it out of his pocket and handed it to me. He said he trusted me to do the right thing if he should die.'

'So what then?' asked Ruben.

'I left. I expect the Little Russian is recuperating somewhere. Who knows if he made it. I should be more concerned, but he has his people too. I'm sure he's fine. All those years ago, they hid the original telegram on a person - the Little Russian - then they hid the person.' Justin continued: 'By the way Dara, nice wig in London.'

Ruben and Dara sat there, trying to take in the way this scene had panned out. What they thought was going to be a simple confrontation had taken several unexpected turns, starting with April's appearance. April had seemed different. Gone was the free and easy demeanour she normally exuded, instead she was sullen and serious.

The most perplexing thing to Dara and Ruben was that Justin barely had a reaction to his wife suddenly reappearing out of the blue. Dara had been worried sick about her. Justin, apparently, had not. At least she could be relieved in the knowledge that April was alive, but she still had a lot of questions and was concerned about her change in character, a character more akin to Dara's.

'Why would April want the telegram?' added Ruben.

'Presumably to give to Geoffrey. Geoffrey and Ethan are supposed to be working together,' replied Justin. 'But there's no love lost between them.'

'But Ethan burned the telegram in front of our very eyes. What if he finds out that the original is still out there,' asked Ruben.

'I doubt they'll tell him,' replied Justin. 'Maybe they don't work so closely together after all. Anyway, it's not our concern. Let's leave them all to it.'

'I guess,' said Ruben.

Eventually Ruben broke the silence: 'Dude.' he said to Justin. 'That's your wife, man, and all you did was sit there?'

'You don't understand,' Justin replied. 'I know I said I'd not seen her, but she has been in touch. I thought she was in the South of France. She left a message to say she was coming back to "do the right thing," continued Justin, his voice starting to rise in pitch as he was starting to understand that things were not as they seemed and panicked about the uncertainty of this.

'A message?' cried Dara. 'But she never answered her phone when I rang. It was a disused number.'

'She doesn't have that phone,' explained Justin. We have a secret way of communicating and let me know where she'll be. It's called the land line. Three rings for her folk's house on the Riviera. It's a peaceful place, away from it all. A chance to hang out and chill. It's our sanctuary and a place to be ourselves without all this. I'm heading down there tomorrow. Why don't you come too? Surely it's time we all deserved a break, now it's over.'

'Why don't we come?' said Ruben sarcastically. He shot a look at Dara who seemed okay with the idea.

'April wants you to come, I know,' said Justin. 'She wouldn't have revealed herself with you here if she didn't.'

CHAPTER TWENTY-EIGHT

It was a calm and still day as Ruben and Dara rose from their bed in Berlin for the last time. They were going home - at last back to America and their now not so familiar life. Before their return they decided to take Justin up on his offer of spending a few days with April and Justin at their home in the south of France. Prolonging their return to the rest of their lives, bridging the gap between high adventure and the welcome tedium of normal life with the excitement of a vacation but without the drama.

It felt strange but it was time to go. There was a certain melancholy in the air but only for sentimental reasons. An unusual situation which had become familiar that was soon to be over. Like an over extended vacation, too much fun can be exhausting, it has to stop at some point. As Douglas, Ruben's boss back at the *Aurora* used to say: *Call the Police, we're having too much fun.* There was a sadness about going but a relief to return to the usual way of living. At least there was something to look forward to, a short stop along the way, a change of scenery – this time with a definite and short time limit. A week away, in the South of France. A different pace of life. Instead of the grey city life and weather they'd have sunshine and flowers, sea and woodlands to explore. A real holiday. It was something imminent to look forward to before returning home to commence the rest of their life.

It was Ruben who got up first, got dressed straight away and went to the kitchen to make the coffee. He was slow and steady, making the breakfast in a deliberate and measured way.

First, he took the coffee out of the cupboard, then opened the drawer and took out a spoon. He scooped a couple of spoonfuls into the cup and placed the cup into the machine, clicking the cup into place. He switched on the button and let the machine do its job. Then he got some slices of bread out of the packet and put them into the toaster, pushing the button down which made the bread disappear inside the machine as it cooked.

Dara and Ruben had grown partial to a full English during their stay, so while waiting for the two machines to finish their tasks, Ruben placed some bacon, tomatoes and sausages under the grill. He realised the sausages would take longer to cook so he cut them in half lengthways and put them back with the others. Meanwhile he heated some oil in a pan and cracked one egg after the other into it, watching and hearing it sizzle then steam as though breathing out a deep sigh of relief.

It was customary for Ruben to be rushing around like a headless chicken panicking that he would miss the train, would not be able to get a taxi, get stuck in traffic. Anything that could go wrong, however unlikely, was definitely going to happen. But Ruben had changed. They were taking a flight back home - and a plane waits for no man. But Ruben knew they could simply get into a taxi that would get them to the airport exactly on time. There really was nothing to worry about. They were just catching a plane, like a million other people do every day.

Dara slipped out of bed and had a shower. It was pleasant to hear the sounds of cooking coming from the kitchen: a gentle bang, a hiss, a knock, a quiet thud. She pottered around the bedroom in her dressing gown, rearranging the contents of their suitcase until Ruben announced breakfast was ready.

They ate in relative silence, savouring the moment, trying to take in as much as possible so as not to forget their temporary home. Dara left the table to dress as Ruben cleaned and put away the plates as carefully as he had made breakfast, checking them thoroughly, making sure nothing was written on their undersides. Dara went into the bedroom, took off her robe to dress and left it on the bed, perhaps to leave an impression of herself, a shadow, an outline of where she once laid to rest.

The taxi came and glided to the airport on this glorious day full of sorrow and hope. Sorry to leave Berlin, and the nightlife, museums and history, sorry to leave Emilia, Ethan Maxim, and all the other people they had met on their adventure. And, of course, sorry not to know the fate of the most curious of them all: The Little Russian.

But alongside the sorrow, there was hope. Hope for the future in every way.

They didn't have what they came to collect, if bringing the telegram home was ever their task in the first place. There was a slight sense of an anti-climax for them both, even though they were still being paid the same amount. It was just a piece of paper, after all. Gone in a flash of a small flame. Yet it was so significant that people were prepared to pay, to die or to be killed for it. But now its voice was silenced and existed only in memories of the few knew its contents. Perhaps they were a little nervous as they hadn't finished the mission themselves but were happy with the knowledge that at least it wasn't in anyone else's hands. April would see to that. The Russians must have been hacked off, their leverage gone for good, but there was nothing to be done and they knew it. But there would be something else in its place shortly.

'We would know if they had it,' Ethan had said. 'They would delight in telling us.'

Dara agreed, trusting implicitly in April to do - as Justin had said - 'the right thing.'

Dara and Ruben were also resigned for their adventure to be a secret, to be dispersed in the winds of time. Perhaps it was time to move on and leave the past in the countries they once were, as neither Germany nor the USSR existed as they had once. German reunification and the downfall of Communism saw to that.

Justin was, perhaps, the most embittered at this as the past was a matter of principle for him, as well as his concern for the present. Or perhaps it was for the purpose of saving the future that the past should be swept out from under the carpet for all to see.

April didn't care either way. She wanted the quiet life now. Their excursion to the south of France together would bring a certain peace to both herself and Justin. Justin reluctantly promised April he would not report a word of what had transpired on their mission to retrieve the telegram, though both knew he'd be thinking of other ways to report the story in some journal some day. April was beginning to wonder what the point of all the secrecy was. Who were they working for, really? Who were they protecting, and why? Being on the right side seemed to be influenced only by where you were born. Who were these sullen Russians anyway? Why were they even bothered? Perhaps one of them might get a medal. A piece of metal to pass down to future generations, or to be discovered in dusty attics in decades or centuries to come, whoever discovered it unable to imagine the magnitude of the impressive symbol in their hand. It really was just a big game, thought April. Everyone just wanted a bit of something to do. Everyone - the British, the Americans, even the Russians - playing at being the spies they saw in films - the glamorous life they yearned for but never found. More exciting than working in the local supermarket, sitting around waiting for customers (or even produce) but sitting around waiting for the person they were tailing was hardly more exciting.

And the Little Russian, institutionalised by a lifetime of hiding, probably went off to live in a cave, April thought. Though no-one would probably ever know what became of him.

On the plane to the south of France, Dara wondered if their adventure had changed them. Would she and Ruben just carry on as usual, eventually forgetting about their experience? Dara hoped not. There was a new-found purpose in her outlook, but she didn't know what that purpose would be.

Ruben looked deep in thought.

'What are you thinking about?' asked Dara, who could hear his thoughts whirring around inside his head.

'The old man, back home. He's selling the cafe,' answered Ruben. I had an email earlier. I don't even know if I'll have a job to go back to.'

'Who's he selling to?' replied Dara.

'He's not found anyone yet.'

'I'm sure the new owner will keep you on, Ruben. You have international experience now.'

Ruben smiled. 'You can never be sure though,' he said. 'You can't be certain of anything these days.'

'Well,' replied Dara. 'Perhaps there's one way of making sure you keep your job.'

'Okay,' said Ruben, cautiously, turning to look straight into Dara's eyes. 'What are you plotting?'

'How much is he selling it for? The cafe?'

'Not sure,' replied Ruben. 'Please don't say what I think you are about to say.'

'Why don't we buy the *Aurora*? We practically ran *The Honey Pot* single handedly with all the coming and going April and Justin did. Think about it. We still have the money for our "couriering" job. You could do the cooking, I'll manage the place.'

Ruben was starting to dream: 'But do we have enough?'

'I don't know,' replied Dara. 'But we have something, and that's a start. We'll find a way.'

'It's worth a shot,' said Ruben, and looked out the window at the sparkling blue Mediterranean.

CHAPTER TWENTY-NINE

Leaving rainy and dreary grey Berlin far behind, Dara and Ruben were greeted by the blue skies and glistening seas of the south of France. Circling the Nice coast gave a lovely view of holiday apartments below and people sunning themselves on the beach. The sparkles made by the sun's rays as they hit the water formed a synchronised dance, welcoming them to this spectacularly paradoxical land. So close to the town was the airport, Dara could almost hear the sounds of the various radios from the beach - a mix of music and jaunty chat breathing life into the corpse-like bodies resting on the sand.

The plane gradually descended, and gently landed right along-side the sea.

Whilst Justin hired a car, Dara and Ruben waited beneath shop awnings intertwined with flowers. At various intervals water sprinklers came up from the grass, often missing the plants and catching Dara instead. Eventually, Justin came with the car. Ruben and Dara loaded their cases into the trunk, and climbed onto the back seat.

The roads were familiar to Justin, but Dara and Ruben looked out of the window with childlike wonderment. Driving down the Avenue Anglaise there were grand hotels on the right and palm trees and narrow beeches to the left. It was different to L.A. which seemed similar but had a sense of nothingness underneath the polished mantle. As they drove away from the town there was a feeling of something even more glamorous and delightful underneath the decorative parasols. It was as if you cracked the icing and dug down, you'd find the most delicious red velvet cake, with the further surprise of smarties in the middle.

The winding roads echoed a gentle fairground ride, swinging and leaning left then right as the car climbed its way up - one side, a deathly drop with nothing in the way of barriers, the other steep, rocky hills. Occasionally, the sea could be glimpsed from above, a sparkling sapphire contrasting with the dusty green and grey of the land.

Up at the top of the mountain they passed through a tiny village comprising a single street with a small convenience store and numerous cafes, a newspaper shop or 'presse', a pharmacy and a small village square with water coming out of a lion's head fountain. Windows and doors almost touched the car as it drove through the village, so narrow was the main street. Ruben and Dara could see the furniture and décor through the window panes, if the shutters were open. It seemed the people didn't mind seeing life here or knowing they could be looked at.

April and Justin's house was near the far end of the village, a little set back from the road. Justin pulled up the narrow driveway, and brought the car to a halt.

'Well, here we are,' he said.

And at the door, waiting for them all with a huge smile, was April.

Inside, the house was light and airy with large rooms and terracotta tiled floors. There was a feeling of relief about the place, as though one could finally breathe. When April opened the shutters at the back of the house, the most stunning view of the mountains was revealed. Numerous peaks went on and on for miles, getting taller and taller, like an opened Russian Doll with all its parts standing in a row.

'That one's Mont Blanc,' said Dara, pointing into the far distance.

Dara and Ruben were shown to their room, and began to unpack, putting their clothes into the quaint built-in wardrobes. Dara opened the long bedroom shutters and a sheet of light flooded the room, revealing a balcony overlooking a field below. Dara stepped onto the balcony, spread her arms out along the balcony rail and took a deep breath, and smiled. The evening sun shone on her face and she felt the rays bouncing off her cheeks. In the field, a donkey shook his head and grunted in an attempt to shoo away flies. Dara went back in to help Ruben put the now empty suitcase on top of the wardrobe at the same time as they heard the sound of footsteps coming up the stairs.

April appeared in the doorway. 'We thought we'd go out for dinner and a drink tonight, if you fancy it. We know a lovely place.'

'Sounds great,' replied Ruben. 'We'll be down in a minute.'

The four of them left the house and walked down a sloping street. Coming the other way, plodding along, was an elderly dog with big floppy ears and an unimpressed look in its eyes. Its mouth was turned down like Alfred Hitchcock, reminding Ruben of a Sherlock Holmes' Deerstalker hat.

'That is definitely a crime solving dog,' he whispered to Dara.

Suddenly taken with the dog, Ruben tried to take a photo. But each time he pointed his phone in the direction of the dog, the dog turned its back. Ruben hid behind a bin and darted out to surprise the dog, but without success. However hard Ruben tried, he just couldn't get a picture of the dog.

At the end of the road, they turned right and reached the square. Just off the square was a small street with a grand restaurant at the centre, covered with ivy and two sets of stairs travelling upwards to either side of the front door. In front of the restaurant stood an iron awning with tables and chairs beneath. A few people sat at the tables drinking pale rose wine out of a carafe and eating baguette slices from baskets. It was a familiar scene that one imagined taking place in villages all over France. A small jazz band were in the process of setting-up just to the left of the tables.

The proprietor came over and greeted April enthusiastically, showing the group to their seats.

'Hey, look at this,' said Dara reading a plaque attached to one of the columns of the awning. 'This was once a fish market.'

Ruben went over to read the plaque more closely: 'So it was, you're right,' he said, a little surprised at Dara's interest.

A waiter came over with menus.

'Un Carafe de Rosé, s'il vous plait,' April said to the waiter.

The waiter answered in English: 'Certainly, madam,' he said, and retreated from the table.

'So what's everyone having?' said April, perusing the menu.

'The *canard* is great,' said Justin. 'I'm going to have that. The *filet de boeuf* is great too. Simple but quality.'

'I think I'll go for the *filet de boeuf*, then,' said Ruben.

Dara pointed to the *thon tartare*, and asked April what it was.

'*Thon* is tuna,' April explained. 'And *gambas* there is raw prawns.'

'Well, I eat raw tuna whenever we eat Japanese back home, so this can't be that different,' answered Dara. 'I'll go for that. What are you having?'

'*Merlin*,' replied April. 'It's a local fish. I've never seen it in England but it tastes so good. You can try a bit of mine, if you like.'

Justin looked up and tried to grab the attention of one of the waiters. Out of nowhere a waiter appeared with their carafe of wine.

'Would you like to try some first?' he said to April, pouring a little of the wine into her glass.

'No thank you,' she said. 'You can just leave it there, please.'

'Are you ready to order?' said the waiter.

'Yes, please,' replied Justin. 'I'll have the *canard*, the gentleman here will have the *filet de boeuf*.'

'And the ladies?' asked the waiter.

'I'll have *thon tartare*,' said Dara, confidently.

'*Et pour mois, le Merlin*,' replied April.

The waiter wandered off with their order, and left Justin to pour the wine. It was so wonderful, thought Dara, to relax, to just *be* - for the first time in a really long time, or even ever.

So relaxed were they, not one of them was aware of someone sat in a car casually watching them with a certain disinterest. The Berlin flat and *The Honey Pot* cafe had been searched, but nothing had been found. The telegram must still be with them - in France. The man in the car thought it too risky to search the house whilst they were here at the restaurant. The house being only a short walk from the square, one of them could have returned at any point, so he decided to keep a watch on them from his car instead.

There would be another time, he thought.

After they'd finished at the restaurant, April, Dara, Justin and Ruben went to the local bar - *Jean's Tonic*. The bar, with its black seating and yellow tiles, looked out of place compared to the rustic old buildings in the village. More 80s retro than French period drama. The ultra-modern DJ equipment looked even more alien. But the place was somewhere to go top off a lovely meal. A few hours later, they staggered back home up the slope.

And the man observed his prey through the cold, steamed-up window of his car, waiting for his moment, wondering what he was doing with his life.

A couple of days later, the man watched Dara and the others leave the house with beach bags and swimming things, seemingly off to the coast for the day. Surely, they wouldn't take the telegram to the beach, so it was bound to be in the house somewhere. And the nearest beach was a drive away.

This was the chance he had been waiting for.

The man watched them drive away, and waited. People often come back having forgotten something, so it never pays to go charging in too quickly. After half an hour, there was no sign of anyone returning, so he decided it was safe to go inside.

The man gingerly walked around to the back of the house and unlocked the back door with his tools, not at all difficult as the old locks were not sophisticated. He looked under every mattress, in every bag and cupboard. He looked everywhere for a safe. But he found nothing. He looked again but still found nothing. There was little point in staying, but on the other hand he would have to report back and return empty handed. So without a further thought, he drove to the next village, found accommodation and headed for the nearest bar.

Traffic moved at snail's pace along the coastal road, but at least it was a chance for Dara and Ruben to enjoy glimpses of the sea between bushes on one side and luscious vineyards on the other. Justin eventually drove down a winding pathway to the beach and the boat club. Neither he nor April seemed to even blink when a black velvet limo drove past.

Being a semi-private beach meant it was more sparsely populated than most others. More curious was the abandoned hotel high up on the hills, its luxury swimming pool at beach level. Iron skeletons that once held the coverings of fixed parasols stood around the pool. The pool itself was empty of water - twigs, stones, old Coke cans and other assorted debris clinging to the bottom. Dara imagined the hotel's glory days - of a pool filled with water glistening in the sun, cloth-covered parasols keeping the burning sun off glamorous hotel guests. People of all ages jumping off their sun loungers and diving into the pool. Their chatter and squeals of delight.

The resort once filled with so much life now standing tranquil and alone.

With the abandoned swimming pool not an option, they made do with what nature had to offer. The group laid down their large, colourful beach towels side by side on the beach, facing the sea. Ruben and April went straight into the welcoming water, while Dara and Justin settled themselves on the towels, preparing themselves for a period of blissful relaxation.

A colossal yacht, black and uninviting, sat anchored in the middle of the bay, a helicopter perched on its huge deck. Smaller yachts and other boats were moored closer to shore.

Not far off stood the sand-coloured houses and rooftops of a nearby village on the other side of the bay.

'What is that, over there?' remarked Dara to Justin, pointing to the village.

'Ah, that's St. Tropez, where the super rich hang out. Or rather those who would like to think they are. It's a strange old town, hectic compared with the stillness of the other villages. It was made famous in the 60s but now it's just people in cafes watching other people, wondering if they are somebody. But no-one ever is. The yachts suggest glamour but really it's ordinary people with too much money, their wives spending their whole lives - and their husbands not very hard-earned cash - in a quest to look identical to their teenage daughters.

Dara pondered on this speech for a moment.

'It's worth going for the freakshow,' continued Justin. 'But that will be a trip for another day.'

For lunch, Justin and April took Dara and Ruben to Port Grimaud where they all ate *moules et frites* in a tacky tourist restaurant on the main square. Port Grimaud was a lively place built in the 60s for people with boats and the leisure time to enjoy them. As they ate, a middle-aged drunk woman in a white floating dress staggered past, up and down and back again. From high up, a semi-naked young lad opened his window and stood out on his balcony for a minute or so, before going back inside. Ruben wondered what these people were doing or even thinking. Each apartment or house had a mooring for the various sized boats, ranging from small fishing boats to large gawky yachts.

After the late lunch it was time to return to the house, via the local Hypermarket - *Le Clerc* - to get some food for the rest of the week. The place was huge. Like the size of *Costco*. Dara had never seen such a variety of vegetables. She counted ten varieties of zucchini, in yellow as well as green, twenty types of tomato in various colours - including black - and fish she had never heard of. Then she came across the grossest thing of all - the meat section - filled with all sorts of animal parts

'Oh my god,' Dara said to Ruben, who also looked horrified. 'Sheep brains! Who the hell would eat that?'

'We eat every other part so why not the brains,' joked Ruben, grabbing Dara's head and doing his best B-movie zombie impersonation.

Driving back to the house, Justin stopped off at what appeared to be a dusty roadside pitstop. In fact, it just sold wine. Not by the bottle, but by the barrel. Since leaving the States, Ruben and Dara had spent so many times looking at the new worlds in which they found themselves in either open mouthed wonderment or simply confused. This was one of those times. There were three flavours of rose for sale that, according to Justin, everyone in the south was drinking. A woman behind the counter gave Dara and Ruben tasters of each, pouring not from a bottle, but from something like a beer tap. They loved them all. The woman went on to fill three glass five-litre barrel-like bottles with each of the wines. Ruben wondered how they would manage to get through it all, but then he'd seen so many people around here drink enormous amounts of the stuff with every meal, but still not get drunk, he realised drinking it with food was probably the sensible thing to do.

After a day in the sun, they sat on the terrace back at the house quietly chatting.

'I've never seen such huge yachts,' remarked Dara. 'And in the middle of the sea. How do the owners get to them?'

'That's what you buy if you're a multi-billionaire oligarch,' answered Justin. 'Common millionaires have smaller yachts moored at the harbour at St. Tropez.'

'I'd love to go to St. Tropez before we leave,' said Dara. 'Wouldn't you, Ruben?'

'We'll take you there, on market day,' said April. 'It's a bit touristy but at least it's something to do.'

'Thank you, April,' said Ruben. 'That'll be great.'

'Yes,' said Dara. 'Thank you, April. And April, those vegetables in the shop were amazing!'

'So many colours,' said Ruben. 'And so many varieties. You just don't get that back home where everything is grown *en mass*. I mean, a zucchini back home is a zucchini, over here you can have any colour you want, practically.'

'In the States, you can have any colour you want, as long as it's green,' joked April.

Ruben laughed with the others, then got up and went back into the house to get some more wine, but the barrel they'd been drinking from was empty.

'It's all gone,' he told the group. 'I can't believe we've got through all that.'

'It was *so* good,' replied Dara. 'I don't normally like wine, but this is, it's like nothing, I've ever tasted - not too sweet, like a dry white but not at all potent. I could drink it forever.'

Ruben picked up the wine glasses from the table and returned to the two remaining barrel-like bottles of wine in the house, unscrewed the lid of one and poured everyone a glass.

No-one really mentioned the activities or grievances of the recent past. To bring it up would have been to spoil the atmosphere - the break from the exhausting experience they had been through. Perhaps this game of espionage would be one they would never be able to escape, no matter how hard they tried. Whilst Dara considered the thought weird and slightly unnerving, she decided to just enjoy the rest of the night.

The morning sun shone through the shutters, casting bright shadows of light into the darkened room, gently waking Dara and Ruben. Dara went with April to the village bakery - *La Patience Fraxinoise* - to get the morning croissants.

There was only one croissant left in the window when they got there - three less than April needed. April spoke in horror to the shop assistant in French, but all became well when the woman behind the counter opened the oven door behind her and produced the next batch.

'Best croissants in France,' April told Dara.

When Dara tried one of the croissants back at the house, she realised April was right. it was so soft and full of flavour, disintegrating in her mouth, leaving a trail of loveliness behind. This was nothing like the dry, cardboard texture and flavour of the croissants she bought back home to have with her coffee in an attempt to feel sophisticated.

After breakfast they set off for St Tropez. They needed to leave early so as to avoid the worst of the long queues into this paradoxical mix of quaint former fishing village and party town. Finally, they found a place to park. Walking along the seafront they passed large yachts moored in haphazard rows.

'It's almost impossible for a plastic boat not to look tacky,' Ruben said. 'Even the one in black out there.'

In one of the concession stands along the front a lone tanned man, short, stocky and dressed in white danced away to Eurodance music blaring from a boombox by his feet, seemingly oblivious to the morning crowd.

'I wouldn't mind sitting down, with coffee or something,' said Dara, exhausted just looking at the dancing man.

So the four of them settled down for a coffee at *Cafe de Paris* and watched the people go by.

Thin wrinkled women in their 60s, dressed in out-of-date Chanel - the exact replica of their sulky teenage daughters tagging along behind. All of these people wandered around as though looking for someone, perhaps hoping to spot an old-fashioned star who promised to attend but never came. St. Tropez wasn't so much stuck in a time warp or searching for times lost, more a place that wanted to break free of its past glamour and live out its old age in peace. Even the moored yachts seemed lost at sea or fed up with the chains holding them. After paying nine Euros each for their *citron presse*, they all left for the market.

On their way back, the four friends stopped off at the ruins of Grimaud castle, and watched a concert of a French pop singer they'd never heard of sing amidst the gloom of the setting sun.

198

CHAPTER THIRTY

EPILOGUE

Along the path by the river Rhône, Katy ambled along, looking around her at the familiar trees and bushes. Katy lived in France but was originally from Hungary - a place to which she would never return. She lived on a longboat moored on the river and divided her time between her home and her art studio in Marseille. A peaceful life without television and a radio hardly ever used. The sunsets were her cinema, the sounds of nature, her soundtrack.

As she reclined on the deck of her long boat, Katy listened to the gentle rustles of the trees conversing. She watched the evening's sunset from her boat, the setting sun masked in part by plant life, scattered the skyline. Very different from the sunset on the shores of Marseille which laid itself bare in solitude, reclining in a sky of bright blue before sinking down into the folds of the sea for a good night's rest.

Along the path came a visitor, April.

April was from England, though now lived in Berlin. Katy had never been to Berlin or to England. These two unrelated people - Katy and April - could never have met. But here they were, together. They were sort of related, albeit so tenuously it went unnoticed, even by those who pursued April and her husband - pursuers who, at this very moment were laying in wait for Justin at a gig in London. The stepdaughter of your birth father's cousin's second husband is unlikely to raise any quizzical expressions. The link was obscure but, nevertheless, present, if only by a thread, barely visible, or like the flapping wings of a butterfly only audible when you know it's there. If you don't see it, all is silent.

April and Katy had met many years ago, just the once. A family visit one Christmas. Katy and April bonded immediately. Being children, though, they didn't keep too much in touch after that, just family news, and the like. There were no more visits, but Katy now lived in the South of France - where April also had a holiday home.

Katy welcomed April to her home, and they chatted a while, looked at the trees and watched the sun go down, both eventually falling asleep to the peaceful rocking of the boat on the river.

The next morning before she left, April gave Katy a small box and a key on a necklace chain.

Katy wasn't usually a curious type but she did have a look at the box April gave her. Unsurprisingly, the key on the chain opened the box. Katy briefly looked at the yellowing telegram inside. But that is as far as Katy's curiosity took her. She put the telegram back in the box, closed the lid and secured the lock. She then tossed it among her other bits and bobs of jewellery and trinkets, putting the key on her keyring amongst the others for her boat, her bicycle and anything else that needed a key. She would keep the telegram a secret - as April had asked - but it really wasn't of any interest to Katy. How could it be? A leaf on the tree that arched over her boat had more meaning and impact, especially when it fell onto the deck and she watched it dance.

So the secret, like many other secrets, is left in plain sight, as all hiding places are. You just need to know where to look. Secrets do not want to remain hidden forever. But if left too long, secrets will find a way of making themselves known. Secrets - like all things - yearn for an opportunity to tell their story.

And, eventually, their story will be told.

THE END

Printed in Great Britain
by Amazon

14998103R00120